Two Tales
Jamali Kamali
and
ZundelState

GUERNICA WORLD EDITIONS 88

Two Tales

Jamali Kamali
and
ZundelState

Karen Chase

GUERNICA
World
EDITIONS
TORONTO—CHICAGO—BUFFALO—LANCASTER (U.K.)
2025

Copyright © 2025, Karen Chase & Guernica Editions Inc.
All rights reserved. The use of any part of this publication,
reproduced, transmitted in any form or by any means, electronic,
mechanical, photocopying, recording or otherwise stored
in a retrieval system, without the prior consent of the publisher
is an infringement of the copyright law.

Guernica Editions Founder: Antonio D'Alfonso

Michael Mirolla, editor
Cover design: Allen Jomoc, Jr.
Interior design: Jill Ronsley, suneditwrite.com

Guernica Editions Inc.
1241 Marble Rock Rd., Gananoque (ON), Canada K7G 2V4
2250 Military Road, Tonawanda, N.Y. 14150-6000 U.S.A.
www.guernicaeditions.com

Distributors:
Independent Publishers Group (IPG)
600 North Pulaski Road, Chicago IL 60624
University of Toronto Press Distribution (UTP)
5201 Dufferin Street, Toronto (ON), Canada M3H 5T8

First edition.
Printed in Canada.

Legal Deposit—First Quarter
Library of Congress Catalog Card Number: 2024944534
Library and Archives Canada Cataloguing in Publication
Title: Two tales : Jamali Kamali and ZundelState / Karen Chase.
Names: Chase, Karen, 1943- author. | Container of (work): Chase, Karen,
1943- Jamali Kamali. |
Container of (work): Chase, Karen, 1943- ZundelState.
Series: Guernica world editions (Series) ; 88.
Description: Series statement: Guernica world editions ; 88
Identifiers: Canadiana 20240443373 | ISBN 9781771839419 (softcover)
Subjects: LCGFT: Poetry.
Classification: LCC PS3553.H3346 T86 2025 | DDC 811/.6—dc23

Contents

A Note	1
Jamali Kamali	5
Part One	7
Part Two	23
Part Three	35
Part Four	47
Notes	*65*
ZundelState	69
1/ Junkyards	71
2/ Brain-O-Mat	103
3/ DNA	113
4/ DuoDreaming	137
5/ Pavel	163
Acknowledgements	185
About the Author	186
Also by Karen Chase	187

A Note

Inside this volume you will find two tales that seem different on their face—but the works are a pair. *Jamali Kamali* is an epic poem that takes place hundreds of years in the past. *ZundelState* is a novella in verse that takes place hundreds of years in the future.

Jamali Kamali was inspired over a decade ago during a writing residency in India. There, I visited the small, stunningly beautiful tomb where Jamali and Kamali are buried side by side in two white marble graves. The red and blue circular ceiling is decorated with sunbursts and floral forms carved in plaster. A band of Jamali's verses encircles the ceiling. According to Delhi's oral tradition, the men were homosexual lovers. Jamali was a sixteenth-century Sufi court poet and saint, and Kamali's identity is unknown.

After visiting the men's tomb, I began, to my surprise, to write as if I were Jamali speaking to Kamali. The imaginary sound of their voices came over me and propelled me forward. Seeing the beauty of their graves, hearing the tale that had been passed down, spurred me on to invent a story of love, sex, separation, and death. It is not based on any historical record—there isn't one.

I wrote one section during a month in Nova Scotia on Cape Sable Island, living in a trailer overlooking the ocean as the fog came and went. Mostly, I wrote at home. It didn't matter where I was. Whatever was in front of me, leaves blowing or a bird hopping, appeared in the poem. A year and a half passed, and finally Jamali and Kamali had had their say. The book was done.

In 2011, *Jamali-Kamali: A Tale of Passion in Mughal India* was published in India, and I returned to Delhi for the book launch. As I read from the book, the men's voices filled the room. Afterwards the moderator, a well-known cultural figure, opened a discussion by attacking me. "You distort history by fictionalizing it!" he said. In answer, I talked about the place and power of the imagination.

To me, at that point, it was clear that fact and fiction were two separable entities. I wasn't "distorting history," I was inspired by a snippet of history to make up my own story and saw no conflict. It wasn't as if my fiction would alter the historical record.

That's what I thought until, a few years ago, I looked up my book on the web to see how it was faring and found myself on a travel portal to Delhi. I was reading about the historical monument, the Jamali Kamali Mosque and Tomb—which subway to take for your visit, opens at sunrise, closes at sunset, Thai restaurant nearby—when I landed on something unexpected.

> *Jamali Kamali* offers a fine piece of structural design
> and a fascinating story behind it.
> **Forlorn Love**
> *After his death in 1535, Jamali was buried in his tomb
> alongside Kamali. Very few are aware that both these
> men were deeply in love with each other. In Jamali's
> poetic works you can find passionate words and phrases
> describing his immense love for Kamali such as "On the
> map of your body, there is nowhere I would not travel."*

The "fascinating story" behind the monument is a fiction. It comes from my imagined poem, not from historical facts. Jamali did not write the line quoted above. I did. The webpage relates a few details about Jamali's life as if they are facts, but the details are taken from my invented poem. The website suggests my book, *Jamali-Kamali: A Tale of Passion in Mughal India,* to learn more about the men's histories. I immediately emailed the people at the website and asked them to correct their mistake, which they did. Relieved to have set things straight, I thought that was that.

I was wrong. To this day, my fictional lines about Jamali and Kamali continue to infect the historical record. I no longer try to correct the errors because I have come to see history as a polluted conglomeration of fact, fiction, and truth.

In my poem, Jamali pictures centuries to come when people will see him and Kamali buried together and know they were lovers. Who is to say if this is fact, fiction, or the truth?

* * *

As Jamali looks to the future from sixteenth-century Delhi, Joe, a main character in *ZundelState*, looks to the past. The year is 3090 when he visits Socrates right before his death because everything that ever happened is still happening. They have much to discuss. Time is bent, warped, and vertical, as opposed to the tidy horizontalness of a timeline.

While Joe and his love Marianna—both outsiders—wrestle with threats from The State, one might hear echoes of Jamali and Kamali from centuries earlier. Time becomes fungible.

ZundelState is a brand-new work. How its contents intersect with history will unfold as time moves forward. In its pages, both factual history and fictional history make their appearance. Factual: James Watson has a dream in which he sees two snakes twisted around each other with their heads at opposite ends. His discovery of the double helix—the structure of DNA—grows from this dream. Fictional: Albert Einstein invents a gene that contains the ability to dream. In the era of ZundelState, the ability to dream has almost disappeared.

So often, writers are advised to "write what you know." In both tales, I did the opposite. Opening oneself to the unknown paves the way for a large-scale exploration rather than the up-close, confining details of "what I know." The unknown is a wider plain—a big, flat, open space where options flourish. It expands the smallness of "what I know." This largesse leads to a place where fear, desire, sadness, and surprise abound. Both *Jamali Kamali* and *ZundelState* are love stories that encompass love in all its forms as the stories unfold in this boundless space.

JAMALI KAMALI

Part One

Just off busy Mehrauli–Gurgaon Road in Delhi, India, the 16th century Sufi court poet Jamali is buried in a tomb next to Kamali, of whom the printed matter says "identity unknown," but who helpful guides say, according to oral tradition, was the poet's lover. Little about them is known.

In the plump dusk, I hear
a peacock screech,
eye marks on my lover's neck.

Kamali, let's go
to the lake
to moisten our love scars.

I will wash mud from
your muscled legs.

My secrets rest
in the wedding
hut. I visit another
man as the moon
circles down.

Come my protégé,
my Kamali, to bed.
I will show you
moves of a new
planet like no
astrologer could.

Bonfires blaze
in Delhi's winter.
While dogs howl
I remove your kurta,
your trousers, to teach
you pyrotechnics.
I am not called Professor
of Fire for naught.

The donkey is caught
between two worlds, as
am I, as are you.
Last night I dreamt of two
princes at play.
Vehicles passing both ways
will praise our marble tomb.

*

When we were boys
I watched you draw
under the shade of
the champa.

I watched you
in the forest
as you herded
goats, twenty,
thirty of them,
maybe even more,
prancing behind you
as I wished to.

Under the eyelash moon,
I watched you gaze
skyward. Will I ever
take you and when,
I wondered.

Rehearsing for us,
I watched the kingfisher
consume the lizard.

*

The grass green male
parrot sports a dark
pink collar.
I have ordered the stitchers
to sew one for us, each.

At cow dust hour,
meet me in the orchard.

Like birds, we'll raid
the neighbor's guava trees.

Our hidden
ravishments roil
inside. I see your
sister, a new bride,
chirping with
pleasure. How long can
we go on like this?

Pleasure-making
couples parade
the fog-laden streets.
I long for you,
lowing with grief.

Kamali, where have you gone?
Have you told our secret?
Let's meet by the stream
near the bamboo grove.

*

Bonfires burn
on every street.
One day I will
startle you,
circle you, as you huddle
for warmth,
to show all our attachment.

When you watch me dance
with the marigold clad
beauty of our town,
do not grieve my boy,
it is you I am picturing.

It is you who will
be buried with me
in twin marble graves
high on the hill.

It will be too late
for any to object.
Let them say
what they will.
And for centuries, if they want.

*

Tonight the boatman will row
us to the island where
he has fixed
a feast and a bed
so soft, my friend,
we will never be the same.

Our secret is safe
with him.
I paid him in sapphires.

Tomorrow I must go
to far-off lands,
leave my winter quarters,
carry the spice-box
south.

Young men
with brooms
brush away the plumeria leaves.
Such sweeping will go on
when I am gone.

For sport,
watch the wiry mason
collect water in the
central well. How he
descends the stairs
with his pitcher,
then flies up.

Do not speak with him.
I beg you.

When men brush the warming ground,
do they sweep the
serpent spirits out too?
Dust plumes up into the hot air.

Do you hear the steps now
of my uncle's prize horse?

It is nearing time to part.
Fog falls through my loins.
Like a pubescent girl, I hanker
for your chest, lost.

Look! The field is
filled with white cranes,
migrating witnesses to our lust.

*

Kamali you anger me.
Go. The men will give
you a broom. Sweep
the sagwan leaves
from my courtyard.
Join the roomboys.

Your moaning is of no use.

Take heed.
I have my eye on the young
mason, his onyx eyes.
His lengthy fingers
will do me good.

I shall shatter
the tiles of heaven
to illustrate how
you peeve me.
A pile of red and blue shards.

My love for you
and hate are large.
One day I consume you,

the next,
regurgitate.

And you?
You seem to waver, as well.

*

Nights filled with massive
thunderbolts, dreams of rival
women and men.

Violet sky, blue doors,
green on the girls' attire –
all praise Delhi's colors.
Your lovemoves pale the palette.

In the humid fields, our odd audience:
a tiger here, a squirrel there.
Cheetahs, too, appear curious.

You say, Kamali, you dreamt
of bolts of velvet,
carmine clothes for us
both. Does this portend
good luck?

Who is the peacock
here? One day you are,
then me.
I love our shifting
plumage, also
how the peafowl
guard us from intruders.

*

What happened?
Like a serpent eagle
attacked, I am featherless.
Your fierceness, Kamali,
is catastrophic.

Your smooth royal fingers,
your rajah-like stance, bore me.
Seasons aiding the goatherd,
your practiced milking hands,
your humbleness I love.

Tonight you must do
as I say. Dress
as my bride. I will walk
through Delhi's streets
with you unafraid.

Then I will regale you
with rubies.
Camphor, aloe wood
will perfume our tent.
No amount of liquor
could make us so drunk.
I promise.

Your sisters watch you,
I can see.

*

Monsoon winds
hurl the buttresses,
wind chimes
crack to smithereens,
I surrender order.
Take me in your arms.

You drain my plan
to go off with the others,
mount my horse.
I am like a small child.

Kamali, I must leave tomorrow
and you must stay.

Turn over.
I will take you now.
Our love calls will
inflame god and goddess alike.

You said you told that girl in the red sari
go home to your mother.
Please tell the one in turquoise too.

*

Ah! I heard you carousing.
The soaking courtyard let loose
with laughter.
Do the roomboys ply
you with wine?
Do others know your
serpentine beauty?

The slave king Balban
has his fine tomb.
Who will see our
monuments to love
when we are gone?
What will they say?
You were my wife?

Down the hill,
goats roam the muddy streets.
A girl walks two monkeys on a leash.

*

It is time, my student,
you learned
the songs of birds:
paradise flycatcher,
the grey hornbill.

After the hysterical rain,
the streaked laughing thrush
claims his turf again.
Kamali Kamali I sing
as I claim mine.

Are you keeping
something from me?
Have you entered
private palaces before?

Fortified walls
do not compare
to your fortified face.

Go now.
I have lost patience.

You say I tire you?
You tire me.

Pillars, cloisters,
floods everywhere,
parapets, moats –
I don't care.

Mausoleum, mosque, tomb too.

I don't know what to make of this.

Gossipers tell
of snakes with beards,
milk, the only way
to appease them.

If we go on,
they will cart me to the
madhouse.
Your legs, for example,
make me insane.

*

No night is long enough,
no season, no year.
We have come to
another winter in Delhi, and
I drive with desire, still.

The hunt begins tomorrow.
I shall go. You stay
and tend the court.
With every stab to leopard
or fox, I lose verve.

Is it the fog?
Wind rocks the jacaranda.
Again, bonfires burn.
Your body cocks the world
out of focus.

I am torn.

A donkey on the road.
An elephant.
My friends together.
Trout from the
northern hills.
The Yamuna.
Nothing interests me.

A battered statue by
the mosque. Two
feet remain, the rest
is dust.

Did you see the slobbering
puppy? Its mother killed
a peacock
as I would, for you.

Never able to share a table,
what will become of us?

I have left you a letter
regarding this
in the niche at Balban's tomb,
the ink, a sea of illegibleness.

Like a prisoner,
one arm gone,
then the other,

I am injured.
Kamali, you ask me why,
your brow a map of wondering.
For you silly man, this putrid
pail of sorrow.

Feverish,
I must take to bed.
My face, my buttocks burn.
I say, ban the arsonist.

A squirrel peers
into my doorway,
sees this clump
of man.

The men wear red shawls
and blue turbans today.
A sea of hues crash.

Again, an orange fog has come.
Where have you been, Kamali,
are you a whoremonger?

Why is your head
always in my books? Storms are
heading south from the Himalayas.
Gather your belongings,
we will do some traveling.

Tonight we will study maps
by the light of my oil lamp,
to educate you
in more ways than one.

I ordered the kheer
drugged with love potions.
Have some.

On the map of your body, there is
nowhere I would not travel.

Part Two

Throughout the reigns of Sikandar, Lodi, Babur and Humayun, Jamali's travels take him to Syria, Iran, Baghdad, Ceylon, Mecca, Herat, Damascus, Palestine and Spain, making for many separations.

Hot wind blasted my torso
with dust as I left Delhi
reeking of beauty.
Stunned by my zeal for you,

I passed a junkheap:
terracotta horse head,
clay arm near a bush.
I slept in a field

of gallardia, red-streaked
like pixie flame.
"What is this place?"
I quizzed a peahen.

Dragonflies seemed to listen.
Before our bond, Kamali,
I pitched into motion.

In the stinging sky,
I rode on to Gujerat,
eyes on the windy horizon,
the smacking smell of dulse,
gulls crisscrossing the universe.

I sailed south to Ceylon,
the indigo sky adrift with stars,
a luminous tomb roof.
Three days from land
as I ruminated on lovers' tombs,
a mountain came in view.

Through the jungle, I rode
toward Adam's Peak.
Fat leeches
wrapped round my ankles,
thrived in the rank green.

Under a great strange tree
an elephant suckled her newborn
near a turquoise pond.
Lime leaves flapped down.

Rubies glittered
off the river sand
at Ratnapura,
the peak's steep side.
All I pictured was
your butterfly laugh,
your glittering eyes.

Clad in rags, fingers jammed,
I started up the cliff's sheer face.

Overshadower of sky and tide,
Kamali, I yearned to woo you more
the higher I climbed.
They say the Peak
is forty miles beneath Paradise.

*

Wrapped in bear hides,
gummy with ash,
I traipsed on as qalandar.

Dumbfounded, I sat
at the tables of poets,
lay skins on their floors.

To their sense, I spoke nonsense,
unhitched their speech.

They relayed stories,
as I whirled round their rooms.

I gagged on roast camel,
downed bugalamun with zest.

Alien lands, alien food!
my home routine gone –
my own dahl, my own chapati,
horse manure, jasmine.

On the mats of strangers
retching from date liquor,
sick for home.

Such longing was a million
times nothing
compared to no you.
Swathed in fever,
my heart pumped water
rather than red life,
my lips logey as wet cloth.

*

As I sleep in your arms now,
all this long ago,
you lassoo me in my dreams.

27

Your tresses
are making me nervous.

Why are you growing
your locks longer and longer?

Remember how I studied
the ropes and snares of hunters,
remember when I was barely grown,
I shared opium
with long-haired ruffians?

Once the sky
turned a pink so glaring,
a sign,
I vowed to live a clean life.

But wisdom won –
I rode on
with the cup-bearers again.

Tramps practice
love on man, woman,
beast. Their nights know
no measure. Days: rest, recover.
Avoid war, conserve love power.

After a storm one day
I lay on the sand
as sailors repaired our hull,
dreaming of times past.

A beardless boy loved me
in a fervor so wild,
the gusty tent seemed on fire.

You, Kamali—I had to have you.

Now, we're here –
tonight I must write a poem
to praise King Babur.
Then let us don the pink paneled
skirts of dervishes
and disappear.

*

Moonrise, I make
my way to your bed.

As we collide,
sparks turn night to noon.

No rains deluge like you,
no breeze like your breath.

I didn't know I knew
your moves –

then, in a mirror, I saw
you raise your arm,

stir the air,
how—wait –

be still—lie down,
no need to move now.

Light starts to crack apart
the navy sky.

Our staffs hail the air.
Moonset—dash home to my wife.

*

Sometimes you soar through fog,
a low bird.

You appear from the mist,
then you are gone.

You face is a field
of light. The denseness,

no veil to vision.
Nothing can pale your plumage.

Wind breezing air, weather!
the wide-faced sea is for me.

But an inland room even more –
you, me and debauchery.

I ponder the Masters, stand on my head,
stumble about like a mute.

I do not mock those who
celebrate grand boulevards

to Heaven—thigh, face, neck.
Why, though, elaborate what is plain?

Genitalia and anus lead nowhere.
Love stops short in their presence.

*

Today Kamali—a lesson
in meteorology.
Fog moves across
the screen of sky.

P'teer, p'teer, p'teer.
The Plaintive Cuckoo
disappears.
The mist, a canvas for you.

Black fog obscures ceiling,
east, west, floor.
Am I standing on my head?
I love you more and more.

Let's play cards tonight.
Who will win, who will lose?
Afterwards, "fetch the ropes"
one of us will say.
Our bond will pump God's blood.

*

Why are you going North?
Is the answer, Kamali, unspeakable?
Are we shipwrecked?

The Masters think
love kills disease.
When I can't have you,
I am sick.

I am crazed.
I am speaking with animals,
eating grass.

I am wearing hooves on my feet,
I dance a khattak to charm the beasts.

"Fishy," I say when I come to a pond,
"we have much to discuss about love."

*

Fog covered berry and bush,
settled on the tamarinds.

Ghostlike and slow,
a shade strolled
across the mango orchard.
The mass paused,
looked to be a bear
on hind legs.

"That is Kamali,
your friend,"
someone snickered.

When the figure moved,
I knew you were home.

Is it shadows you love?
Let's go to the yard.
Tell me everything, Lovebird.

*

While you were gone,
I feasted at the King's table.
Mirror-like fish slid down my throat.

Under canopies, with ambassadors,
I dined with Uzbeks and Qizilbashes,
loose grass screens cooling us.

Men inflamed elephants, prodded camels.
To amuse us, the beasts fought.

Wrestlers jabbed as acrobats twirled aloft,
daggers and sable wraps were given to guests.
Piles of purses and gold
were given to Babur first.

Did you know he wrote
the story of his life?
Humanyun read the pages.
King Babur loved a boy in his youth.

*

The teasing strapping boy of long ago
bound my limbs to posts,
loved me from behind.
The rain roared ...
it was monsoon time.

Kamali, you tell me a story now.

Let us bend towards God,
unpack the ropes.

You will lose the need to move …
Coo-rooroo-rooroo …
You will turn untame,
stretching, rustling,
ringing with a broad
tenor as court musicians
play the bansari!

We will sponge, soap, and swab.
"Roomboy! Douse us with coco balm!"

*

Coo-rooroo-rooroo –
on the ground this morning
the Panduk courted.

The male Dove
hopped towards
the female's rear.
Motionless, her back to him.
He swelled his feathers,
she flit hers.

Coo-rooroo-rooroo.
He mounted her.
They took their time.

Time to stop moving –
no run, no shift, no glide,
no unquiet from morning to night.

Kamali. Let's stagger towards the paradise of calm.

Part Three

Jamali reminisces to Kamali about the time when Jamali had returned from a hunt and a battle in Mewat, where he had been sent by the Mughal king, Babur.

The sand blew so hard—remember?
we had to take cover.

"How close was the lion?"
you asked.

"Take off your turban,"
I said.

Outside, torn roses blew past.
Butterflies scattered.

Remember how the roof tiles
shook with pleasure?

"How close was the lion?"
you asked again.

My mind roamed to that long ago dusk.
A smokey-eyed boy poled his boat down the Indus.

Later, camped in a tent,
I slept unclothed, alone.

Through the night, I rode a black leopard's lean back, my privates
abuzz in the oleander air.

"The lion was close," I said.

Battle blood from the day before.
A tender boy bled from an arrow strike.

I covered him in my kurta as he died.
Sickened, I rode into the overlit noon,

came on a field of riderless elephants
crazed from gun sound, their soldiers trampled,

common death, everywhere I looked. Before this,
I was sick for you, and home too—now, nothing at all.

I taste apple on your mouth, Kamali,
smell wheat on your chest—you have been threshing!

Winds of the earth fatigue and seas find rest,
the sad, bloody hunts of war and beast recede.

The lion was so close,
I felt his unusual breath.

From all sides, we stabbed the beast.
I saw the lion's heart—his and the soldier boy's,

the same—furrows, auricles, vena cavas, twists,
turns, astounding aortas. After this, how to find life again!

Kamali, love equals life, as man's and lion's heart do.
I knew then, you are my life, my love, my lion, my wife.

*

I journeyed feverish across serpent-filled underbrush,
through monsoon-flooded gullies, made my way

from tomb of this one to tomb of that, then out on the sea
one night, I made a pact with the devilish waves:

for centuries, Jamali and Kamali will rest in graves
inches apart for all to witness.

Tamerlane and Genghis Khan run through King Babur's
blooded veins, but he has a softer side. "Babur,"

I will say, "build a tomb for love of man by man,
as natural as your conquering strain, like any beast's

heartbeat, like the sun coming up." I looked about and
there were stones, so many large boulders of those here

then gone. Straw huts newly appeared one day in a field –
deserted, the next, as Hindus moved along…

What is this looseness to home?
Home moves with one, when there is love.

Our home, Kamali, will be high on a Delhi hill,
our bed, white marble tombs.

*

What has my life been?
I moved as beggar,
as dervish I danced,
wrote verses,
fathered sons,
hunted, battled,
stumbled as tavern straggler,
skinned my knees,
heard a cheetah call,
too dark, too scared, to set up camp,
food finally for the wolves.

I sailed oceans,
I prayed,
watched as the king was given a diamond
worth all the world's commerce of half a day,
and yet as I saw that boy die,
life lacked sense. I beg you now,
Kamali, please speak up –
your silence is slaying me.

*

Trees high on both sides, up
the only way to go,
up the mountain pass.
Sheer incline
heaves down the
rocky cliff.

Chimes ticking the air, and flutes:
commotion on the plateaus.
Faces of dark men
painted as white birds.
In peacock-feather skirts,
they dance.

The alchemous fog falls
fast on the scene.
I stray into the ancient woods
with my soon-to-be-dead father,
hunt leopards together …
drumbeat.

Dusk's pink threads weave into night.
Shaken, alone with the beasts,
thoughts of your flesh,

I ponder the conquering heart's core:
battles, sexual takings
and leavings, predators.

What is love, what is natural?

I pulse through this hourglass world,
tempo of sand fall,
move my boney feet up the pass,
move memory over this planetary surface,
trace of all gone before, and what's to be,
the past shivering alive into now.

Blood pulses through me,
as I pulse through the world,
constant from my black curls
to my brown toes. Up in a tree,
the leopard's yellow eyes light
the lightless night. To myself I say,

Don't be afraid, my boy! When my boyish body
tagged after the goatherd, hoping for a glimpse of you –
men and men! My body holds what I was and am –
know it or not—same heart now, same heart then,
slithering oily from my mother's womb, out
into earth's fragrant winds.

*

My long song comes as sand drops
down the hourglass.

Lion, I call you *lion*.
Your eyes, for one.

41

Your glowering, sundrenched torso,
your muscled thighs,

bronze arms. When you
stretch your arms

towards me, throw your garments
to the floor, recline

on plush cushions, lay
down your sword,

wait, gaze and wait,
time done with …

no battle, nor woods,
nor outdoors at all.

Yesterday the hour sounded, Lion,
 sand descended,

how many years now
me and my wild night lion

moan, glisten, growl?
Who says there's no time

in the beamish fog,
no wolf, no color, no cat,

and here comes nothing like a man.

A dervish?
How mistaken one could be!

A man?
A lion?
A woman?

*

Before Babur, before Humayun,
one long winter ago,
Sultan Sikandar, the ruler,
himself a poet and poet-lover,
crowned me poet of the court.

When he died, Lodi, his son
had many of his father's men
killed off.
I feared death then, or jail.

Snows outside threaten now,
and fear returns.
Inside with you, Kamali, coals.
Rooms with beds swell to world size.

As you sleep,
I guard your limbs,
your chest's heat,
fur of my prize lion.

I am yours as dervish or saint,
in sickness, in health.
I am yours in battle,
or in the thick forest of the hunt.

Out where the hunt happens,
men converge around the lion,
maul the thing, cold light could

strike, thunder approach
and no thing would dampen the kill.

Threat of hunt
threat of battle.
threat of some lockup.

I have lost sight of nature, and danger
lurks over every hill.

*

I dread night, jerk awake.

My breeches stink up the room.

When I hear footfalls,
my dumb heart scrapes:

Pear
Noose
Rose petal

Do crows migrate?

Will men cart me off to jail?

You said you once saw an indigo bird—remember Kamali? –
off-course, like me, in a Delhi garden,
perched on the raggedy cosmos.

Imagine ambling free
between narrow cliffs,
forms like tent whirls
making rookeries.

I can see you crouching on the banks of the Yamuna,
hands under water, ready to clutch the fish.
I see you at the stove, cooking biryani.

Confinement smothers me
like a hellhole.

To picture you is a huge wound.
I refuse tears, not to lose fluid.

Gems came my way,
saffron robes, glorious turbans.
I rode in ivory-covered palanquins,
covered you with purple shawls,
bound you with silken bonds.
My underarm stench now thrills the horseflies,
birds, a lost cause.

To think, you cooked me rice!
To think, your fingers outlined my lips.

Is it snowing?

Oh! delicate powder –
how to breathe if not for picturing.

My mind is paradise,
as time seeps from me.

I hear a bumblebee.

Through my mind's hall,
skulls reek.

I'm the sea.

Remember, Kamali, how snow piled up on Himalayan peaks?

The lion was close,
her footprints showed.

The brush of her coat
spun gold in the sun.

The relaxed lion sunned herself
near the watering hole.

The sundial keeps moving –

Man is wolf to man, a sadhu said –
and the sky—it must be turning red.

Part Four

It is 1536, the Mughal ruler Humayun is in power. Jamali has gone west to Gujarat with Humayun and other warriors, to conquer territory. Kamali speaks.

Through the difficult
air, Jamali,
I speak to you
from afar.

Months have passed.
Still it is you
on the paths,

in the fields.
Your face,
I crave.

The shine
of your black
eyes pulls me

by heat
so fractious and deep
I can't stand straight.

Rattled birds
dart and hit
the frantic air.

I keep seeing a
man's face
on the path

near the bamboo grove.
Hollow cheeks,
taut.

Barefoot
in the branch,
the heart at last.

Wordless Jamali,
do not ask.

Sadness soaks me.

Meager speech.
Blankness –
rash.

In this thicket –
Dragonfly,
take heed.

Your face—sweet
beautyscar
alight.

Jamali, your face …
I'm speechless.
No.

Your eyes are
deep. No.

Words land
loud on the
persimmon tree.

Mouth.
Hip.

I cower.
Words blow like wind.

I cower, Jamali!

I'm chopping wood.

I'm going
to chop
saplings.

*

I taught you weather,
Jamali, and
fog.

I taught you
Great Bear
in the sky,

monsoon —
words
you thought
you knew, I
made fresh.

Then you left.

Birds
sang
single notes.

You have
warred
too much, my

Professor
of peafowl, my

guide
through the palace
of pleasure:

arch
bridge
corridor.

Banners swelling light
as we loved beneath.

Your muskpod –
I need
to smell
your chest.

*

I can't say
Jamali, remember
to fuel our loving.

Once I told you
of the slight crease
below one lover's waist, how
from his navel to his genitals,
soft hair made arrows.

Remember the costumed boy,
cheeks a rush of rose,
and lithe, how
fiendishly he danced
to the lutes,
his feet never still.
I took him to bed,
found he was a girl!

And remember Jamali
that bristly
old man,
scratching his buttocks?

Squatting on the terrace,
slurping his dahl,
he looked up
so kindly,
my heart pumped sugar.

You said
Kamali
will we reach
this lustre?

Soon after, you mounted
your war-adorned elephant,
raised a red triangle flag
and disappeared.

*

Nights now
sleepless.

Gulping water.
Tuk tuk tuk—the owl.

I am dismantled
like glass chips.

You were
the one
who twirled
to pieces.

You,
making your way
through the desert
subject to enemy
and beast.

You are on a pass –
enemy troops
lust for your
heart.

And I
do nothing,
safe in my tent,

a paralyzed pasban
against time
and dark.

In my sleep,
I ride
a giant peacock,
a snake in its mouth.

*

My dead mother
was a dyer of cloth.

Madder, ochre,
alizarin –
breath of wild spice.

Billowing cotton hung
in the wind,
pink dye
dripped to the ground.

I'd never,
I thought,
see beauty
equal to
that wet color

until you,
my Shaykh.

*

From afar,
your sandals removed,
I watched you
run turbanless
through the rose grove,
loose curls
swirling behind.

Your strong back,
head erect,
your long, delineated spine …

I craved you'd want me,
spend your spinning mind
on mine.

*

The air is
filling
with elephant dung,
waking me up.

Curly, black clouds
are circling
the fat, fiery moon.

Drumming.
A horse skids.
Someone here.
Someone's in my tent.

Jamali murda.

Jamali is dead.

*

I'm scratching
the ground,
breathing dirt.
No sky, no star,
only down.

I'll murder
the astronomers.
Keep them away.

Jamali!
You went out
the second door
of the inn!

They are
carting you
home.

Peafowl stumble,
severed
from each other –
no –
they search.

Velvet-saddled horses
come in view.

Thirty or so.

Smokiness.

The horses slow down.

A man says
"Jamali murda."

*

Who
am

I
talking
to?

"Elephants will follow
carrying Shaykh Jamali."

Oh.

Pale yellow petals
pile up by my tent.

People offer apricots.

The tomb, ready.

Birds and drums lamenting.

I want
to sleep next
to your corpse.

You, bathed
of battle blood,
me robbed –
neither bather,
nor soaper.

You washed mud
from my legs once.

I turn the cot-bed
upside down,
throw the tray,

heave the mirror at the stone.

*

No more
will I
throw my arm
over your bony hip

as you dream,
hold your member
in my palm.

No more
will I glare
at your face
as you babble
nonsense.

No more winter spats,
no more song.

*

The horseman lifts
the crimson cotton shroud –
my Shaykh
made small by death.

Jingle of bell.

His shriveling
shell, a piece
of small flesh.
Jamali—you were tall.

Riderless, the sour
old elephant
hauls you.

The tomb, laden
with jasmine and sweets.

Masters prepare
their dance.
Hubbub of
ney,
cauldrons of
fruit
and rice,

the courtyard, full.

You, released
from your body's
jail, villagers feast,
your spirit, free.

No.

Your forehead is gone.
Your eyes are gone.
Gone your cheeks,
your neck.
Gone your chest.

Gone hips,
buttocks, penis.
No more legs.

Your hair—gone.
Your words!
Gone is your voice,
your whisper.

A pubic hair
of yours,
found
in your
bed—this
is my wealth now.

Your tomb—no, our tomb—gleams,
polished red and blue tiles,
white marble graves
buffed to a shine.

Roomboys who brought us
love potions, make
death preparations.

Flute players
line the dust-blown path
to the mosque,

stinging of celebration.
In every niche, candles wavering.

Through the ascending crowd,
I wander down towards mute Delhi.

Pricker bushes brush my legs.
Nightingales lose their song.

61

I thought you'd come to me in dream but you don't.

Leaves on the champa, like torn cloth,
the sky, pink satin,
the ground, linen.
The world, like dyed cloth I will never touch.

Jamali murda.

The jealous hill has you now.

Your sound recedes.

My hands
you loved –
idle now.

I bury my pen
and charcoal
in the ground.

Jamali murda.

I visit the bamboo grove
where we used to meet
by the stream.

Jamali murda,
the mango orchard too.

White cranes
look
for you.

I am sinking.

Birds stream uphill
as I go down.

Goodbye hibiscus.
Goodbye plumeria.

Snow must be falling on the Himalayas.

Wrapped in shawls,
a lemon in my mouth,
I am walking north.

Notes

P. 9: **kurta**—A loose-fitting tunic or shirt, knee-length or longer.

P. 18: **Balban**—The founder of the Slave Dynasty, Balban was the Sultan of Delhi from 1265 to 1290. His dilapidated tomb, very near the Jamali Kamali Tomb, was the first time a true arch was used for support in an Indian structure.

P. 20: **Yamuna**—The Yamuna, or Jumna, is the second-most sacred river in India, after the Ganges (Ganga). It begins in a frozen lake and glacier in the Himalayas, and flows for 850 miles, past Delhi, past the Taj Mahal in Agra, southeast to the Ganges River.

P. 22: **kheer**—Pudding made with basmati rice, milk, sugar, cardamom, ground almonds and saffron.

P. 26: **Adam's Peak**—A mountain in Sri Lanka, formerly Ceylon, sacred to Muslims, Hindus, Buddhists, and Christians. For over a thousand years travelers, including Marco Polo, have made pilgrimages to the peak to see the indentation of what looks like a giant footprint, thought to be put there by Adam, the Buddha, Shiva, or St. Thomas, depending on the religion.

P. 26: **qalandar**—An itinerant Sufi, who learns and teaches during his travels, and who partakes of intoxicants. Qalandars whirl, dance and utter refrains while performing rituals. The 11th century Sufi Baba Tahir wrote: *I am the mystic gypsy called Qalandar / I have neither fire, home, nor monastery. / By day I wander about the world, and at night / I sleep with a brick under my head.*

P. 27: **bugalamun**—Means turkey in modern Persian. In the *Baburnama*, Babur refers to this bird as having *"delicious flesh. In* *winter it descends to the mountain foothills, and if it is made to fly over a vineyard, it cannot fly anymore and can be caught."*

P. 28: **tresses**—In *The Mirror of Meanings*, Jamali explores in verse how parts of the body relate to God, according to the Sufis. *Every step on the road of the tresses is narrow; the world of the tresses is the world of darkness.*

P. 32: **khattak**—A traditional fast-tempo-ed dance, requiring physical skill and performed with zeal.

P. 33: **The** *Baburnama*—tells of Babur's youthful, sexual love of a boy. His son, Humayun, did read his father's memoirs.

P. 34: **bansari**—One of the earliest wind instruments. Seven round holes are bored in a hollow piece of bamboo stick. Some bansari are held straight away from the face while others are held transversely, parallel to the eyebrows as it was used by Lord Krishna.

P. 39: **Tamerlane** and **Genghis Khan**—Ancestors of Babur. The fifth generation on his father's side was Tamerlane and the 15th "degree" from Genghis Khan on his mother's side.

P. 40: **diamond**—Thought by many to be the Koh-i-noor diamond. From the *Baburnama*: *"When Humayun got to Agra, the people of Bikramajit's clan were thinking of fleeing, but the men Humayun had stationed there seized them and held them under guard. Humayun did not let them be plundered, and by their own agreement they presented Humayun with many jewels and gems, among which was a famous diamond Sultan Alauddin had acquired. It is well known that a gem merchant once assessed its worth at the whole world's expenditure for half a day. It must weigh eight mithcals. When I came, Humayun presented it to me, but I gave it right back to him."*

P. 45: **palanquin**—An ornately decorated covered litter, carried on poles on the shoulders of two to six men. Sometimes singers or storytellers entertained the luxurious travelers.

P. 45: **man is a wolf to man**—Plautus, a soldier, a wanderer, and ancient Rome's (254 B.C. approx.) most renowned playwright, said *homo homini lupus.*

P. 54: **pasban**—Persian for the word *watchman*.

P. 55: **shaykh**—Persian word indicating respect for Sufi masters.

P. 57: **second door of the inn**—The world is The Inn of Two Doors, according to the Sufis. We enter through the first door, Birth, and leave via the second, i.e. Death.

P. 60: **ney**—Likely the first pitched instrument. It is an oblique rim blown reed flute with five finger holes in front and one thumb hole in the back.

P. 60: **body's jail**—In the later 13th century, Rumi, the Persian Sufi poet, introduced music and dancing during the funeral rites. He wrote: *When the human spirit, after years of imprisonment in the cage and dungeon of the body, is at length set free, and wings its flight to the Source whence it came, is not this an occasion for rejoicings, and thanks, and dancing?*

ZUNDELSTATE

1/ Junkyards

&&&&
Marianna

I was pubescent.
I slept a lot.
Things were confused and confusing.
I loved to lounge around in my sunflower yellow sweatshirt.
I loved to play my ukulele and make up songs.
I loved hanging out with my friends.
I loved my older brother, he was so cool.
I adored my grandmother.
My mama.
My papa.
I was living my private life as if it was a thousand years ago.
That was inside.
Outside our house, the opposite.
I obeyed the ZundelState.
I was the perfect governmental teen.
Their desire was my goal.
That was fine with me.
I'm sixteen now.
I saw no conflict between my private antiquated home life and my
public stance, standing, and accomplishments.
I was being primed for Apparatchik status in ZundelState's
HistoryShit Division.
A stellar functionary, that's me.

I met Joe Gulogulo a few weeks ago.
He was not my type.
"My sexual prowess is quite something," he announced.
"Remarkable, in fact."

I thought he was weird.
He had just come back home from the Junkyards.

Home used to be where you hung your hat.
It used to be your farm.
Your hut.
Your shack.
Where your father planted a peach tree.
It used to be where you kept your stuff.
Your old books.
Worn-out wallets.
Home used to be a sweet-smelling room.
Words I don't know.
What do they mean?
Wallets?
Hung my hat?

Now Home is private.
It's personal.
It's secluded.
It's cave-like.

Elsewhere is everywhere else but Home.
Elsewhere is ruled by ZundelState, it's public.
It is called Agora.
A-Z.
Proper and particular behavior is dictated in public.
There is no such thing as the self.
No such thing as private.

Home is where members of ZundelState retreat from the Agora.
A sage described members of ZundelState: "At home, people are
like snowflakes, each one unique. Elsewhere, they all match."

The most severe punishment meted out by the State is
homelessness—not execution, not electricity, like in ancient times.
All life is lived in public, everywhere else but Home.
Homeless, there you are, outside fighting the massive snowstorm.
Everything intrudes and it is loud and raucous.
Homesick, your punishment.

Colors are assigned to Elsewhere and Home.
Home is brown, Elsewhere is white.
If you travel light-years out to Starspace, you see confounding
patterns made by the whites and browns.
And you hear faraway singing, "By the rivers of Babylon, there we
sat down, yea, we wept, when we remembered Zion."
The meaning of this spatial musical phenomenon remains a
mystery.

Why does ZundelState permit Home in the first place?

&&&

Kern

Good question, Marianna.
As the narrator of this story, I find this confounding.
Rebellions could rise up.

*

In spite of Joe's weirdness, Marianna got to know him more and
more, and she was surprised.
With a man from Elsewhere, she felt Home through her core.
Nothing like this had happened to her before.
As they listened to each other talk, their eyes crunched up in a
smile, in unison.
The proximity of his body to hers was almost familiarity.
Their language meshed, as if they had heard and learned the same
intonations from babyhood, as if they had been stewed in the
same cauldron.
The magnetism of their incomprehensible shared past acted on
them like a lodestone.

They each had mountains to tell the other.
But it was like they each knew the other's story already.
Home, love, family, all intertwined.
As time extended, when she was not with Joe, she became
homesick.

Marianna was Joe's gal next door.
Every person's Opposite lived next door.
Joe was Marianna's Opposite.
The Opposite made life hard for the person next door.

76

Each reminded the other of what they were not.
When Marianna saw Joe looking dreamy out on his porch, she knew he was in trouble.
She knew he had probably ventured out to the Junkyards in search of traces of history.
By his expression, he looked to have been successful.
And when Joe saw Marianna blissfully, in the warm sunlight, pinning her paintings to the line, he worried for her.
There was no right way.
If art made you gaga, you were haunted by the blank barren past.
But if your life was an ongoing hunt for what had been, each day was not nearly enough.

Marianna was in her yard hanging canvases on the line.
She loved art with the same intensity Joe loved history.
She had clothespins and a laundry line to hang out her paintings.
The sun would beat down on them so they ended up with a fresh smell and a gorgeous color-fade.
To her, at home, art was life.

&&&
Joe

Hello, Reader.
You are reading a book.
Made from paper!
It's Joe Gulogulo here—a lover, a lover of history.
So bear with me as I explain how come you are holding this rare
thing in your springtime hands.

Long ago, an oral tradition began.
People listened to stories on hand-held objects called devices.
A storyteller named Homer proclaimed iliads on devices
while videos of a village called Greece, now buried under the
Mediterranean Marsh, flashed across the screen.
In the remote countryside, a band of poets called Punk Provençals
marched around singing stories to passersby.

But for hundreds of years before that, people had books, stories
written on paper that was abundant as emeralds.
Books, like food, were in libraries and automats.

Which came first, the library or the automat?
Or were they actually the same thing?
People have never solved this conundrum.

Automats had walls with glass and steel compartments and slots
for coins, the wampum of the day.
There were sections with titles like Hot Dishes, Pies.

Standing there, you'd choose what you liked:
For example, the Fruit section had glass-enclosed compartments

which displayed books:
Rubyfruit Jungle
Grapes of Wrath
A Clockwork Orange
James and the Giant Peach
A Raisin in the Sun

You insert your wampum and the door pops open, you pull the book out, put it on your tray, and go sit down at the cafeteria-style table.

You sit alone. No one can sit near anyone else.
That is required for digesting the pages.

The process of eating books might have begun almost by accident in the first half of the twenty-first century.
By chance, I discovered words scrawled on a napkin in one of my junkyard finds.

Digesting Chaucer
A cheap crappily printed on crap paper
paperback reddish orange Bantam Classic of
The Canterbury Tales and I start to read
Whan that Aprill with his shoures sote
The droghte of Marche that perced to the rote
and I keep reading a few more lines
put my mouth around it
take a bite of the book
the pages taste like potatoes

Next day I had a knowledge and grasp of The Canterbury Tales *as if I had spent a year in college studying them. I never realized the power of the word digestion.*

What is *college?*

79

&&&

Kern

When Joe got the notion to travel, on came a bad case of vertigo.
He looked at a fixed point in the room as it was spinning, then
began to gag, and finally Joe vomited.
Each time he traveled, it was a battle.
He'd be torn between turning the heat up high and taking to bed
or flying out fast through the front door, woolly and free.

Today, he was determined to leave home and head west to the
Junkyards, all the way to the ShoeFields.

As Joe got closer to the Junkyard towns, he heard the howling
dogs who guarded the gated zones.
It was late, so he decided to stop at the motel for the night—
always a dangerous choice when he was on the road, because of
the temptation not to leave the motel.

When Joe woke up, he shook his legs to wake them, shook off all
the poison.
And his hands, one at a time—first the left hand—shake, shake,
shake.
Then the right.
His extremities were ready.
He did his stretching regime—opened his mouth wide, let air
blow in to cleanse his innards.

Joe Gulogulo was dreadfully nervous about this trip.
He was focused on reaching the fields of shoes and knew that
seeing the enormous mounds of them would be good, but he was
also anxious that something untoward might occur.

He gathered his strength, got dressed.

Turned the lights out in his room, went to check out of the motel.

When he got to the front desk, there was a pretty woman, ready to assist him.

"Boy, wait till you see what I have for you!" he announced.

He often acted crass on meeting an appealing female.

Nervous.

He handed her the key and she hung it on the wall with the other keys.

He paid her with actual things—coins made out of metal.

In the privileged classes, some people were beginning to use coins as money.

Rumors were starting to circulate that someday people would pay for things with paper, but that was a long way off, paper being what it is, made from trees.

Joe knew that way past the ShoeFields there were fields which contained variety and every once in a while, you came upon a cardboard carton that shed light on history.

It is hard to grasp why Joe Gulogulo had such an overwhelming desire to know the story of how he had come to be who he was, but the answer probably lay in one of those cardboard boxes.

Joe Gulogulo, a distant cousin to the fierce wolverine, the loneliest animal, the fiercest animal, gulo gulo, the small mammal who, for food, could rip large beasts to shreds, held the belief that he could uncover whatever truths were out there.

Once he could get himself out of his house, once he could shake all the poison off his hands and stop his incessant puking, he was free to discover what his story was, whatever it was, his history, history itself.

His recurring shoe dream helped.

He had felt shoe claustrophobia ever since he was a boy.

When he wiggled his toes freely, his appetite was whet for knowledge.

Yes, Joe was on a search, as fierce for history as his namesake was for food.

*

What a trial it was to get past the growling dogs who guarded the Junkyards.
Joe had never been afraid of dogs before, but today, he was more cautious than usual.
He had heard of a dog named Chance, who without warning would bite a person without provocation.
The dog's owners loved their Chance.
They fed him as if he were DogKing of the world, and when he bit people, they blamed the bit person.
"You showed fear," they said, "no wonder you got bit."
One man lost a chunk of his thigh to Chance, one woman had half her vagina ripped off, because sweet, adorable, innocent Chance was curious.
So when Joe approached the Junkyard dogs, he said a short prayer to himself, *Oh god please protect me from these ravenous beasts*, and galloped on through the gates.

He walked and walked towards the ShoeFields.

It was early, the sun beginning to rise, nary a soul in sight.

The main road connecting the fields was made of dirt, and there were large ruts in it.

Joe walked slowly, looking from side to side, enjoying the peace.

The rising light of the sun demolished the starlit sky.

The sky was purple, tinged with thin buttery yellow stripes.

The only things moving, besides Joe, were bands of large white cranes flying across the sky.

When he reached the first Junkyard, he decided to keep walking.

The road made a strong wide curve that he could not see around.

Momentarily, Joe panicked—what was up ahead?

Home home home, that's where I belong and not venturing out into the open place.

He walked forward despite his anxiety.

He liked what he saw, how he felt.

The more he walked, the more he liked it.

Right foot, left foot.

Onward.

Eventually, Joe came upon an EverythingField—chaotic bits and pieces.

He spied a cardboard box under some bolts of cloth.

There were few cardboard boxes in existence, but Joe had a genetic talent for finding them.

With tenderness, cautiousness, and with hesitance, he gathered up the box and trudged back down the road to the gates.

The dogs stopped growling and began to howl, all eyes on Joe Gulogulo.

Joe's stare penetrated each dog—one by one, he silenced them.

They knew they were in the presence of some thing to be respected.

He walked out of the fields, back onto the main dirt road, and headed east, towards home.

&&&
Marianna

I love Joe's brainpower.
I love his chest.
I love how he smells.
He's different from the rest.

When I say *pthalo blue* or *rembrandt* or *horsehair brush*, he doesn't say "Nonsense!"
Joe listens.
He wonders.
He questions.
I want to touch his arm.

He says words to me that neither of us understand.
Like *Crimean War, Google, Christ, Erg.*
Do I say "Nonsense"?
Now I wonder whether he knows what he is saying.
If so, will he ever tell me?

My hair is long, some of it curly and some of it straight.
Brownish/light brownish/blondish.
I don't like the layers.
I'm letting them grow out.
All my clothes are a derivative of dirt.
I never look in the mirror.
I like to make people laugh!
I only wear painter's smocks.
It's good to know how people look.

I'm short.
No, sorry, I'm tall actually.

But this is what I really want to tell you.
This happened when I was nine, going on ten.
One night I lay on my bed and soon fell asleep.
I began to see moving pictures.
I was there, planted in the pictures.
Things made sense but not in the regular way.
Everything was gauzy.
My focus shifted from thing to thing.
One moment I was seeing a small, dark shadow under a chair,
then the shadow turned into thousands of flying insects.
I was immobilized.
Then, a siren.
All of this happened while I was asleep.
In the morning, the motion pictures kept taunting me.
I tried to hold on to them but they vanished.
I forgot about that night after a few weeks.
I had to.

Then—maybe I was fourteen, it was summer—I was falling into a
deep sleep, I could hear a sound, a sound I had never heard before.
But did I actually hear it?
Or was it somehow taking place inside my brain?
When I fell into total sleep, feeling pictures moved through my
vision.
Pictures like clay, like longing, like butterflies, like flight.
When I woke up, nothing!
Irretrievable.

The images gave onto something called "feelings."
I was left with them but not the film story that produced them.

How did those pictures get into my head?
And then they were gone.
Thus began years of longing.
For what?

I never told a soul before and now I'm telling you.

&&&
Joe

I dream of shoes, I dream of books, I dream of high buildings and philosophers.
I dream of a prison cell in the ancient agora sitting with Socrates as he awaits death.
There I am with him.
I dream of getting lost in a huge cornfield, unable to find my way to safety.
I dream of planting a bed of nasturtiums.
They don't come up.
Weeds do.
Weeding the bed with Plato.
Me and Plato glancing back and forth at one another pulling out dandelions.

I dream of traffic coming to a standstill.
Paralysis.
No exit.
On towards death.
I dream of getting frustrated and annoyed with Sigmund Freud, telling him off.
"Do not speak to me that way!"
How did you come up with foot fetishes?
You stupid dope.

I am in the land of rhubarb stalks.
High spikes with white fluffy flowers.
I am pulling rhubarb, my hands near the ground, trying to get a good grip on the stalks.
They keep breaking.

Everything keeps breaking.
So what, I bake a pie.

On the southern US border, I am shooting a rosary stealer in the
head.
Close up. I have a small pistol and shoot chipmunk by chipmunk
until they are all gone.
This is not a dream.
This is a desire.

I am dreaming of Plato, sitting at a table, writing words down.
I am him in the dream, feeling lugubrious.
Please thank me for my wisdom.

I am dreaming of riding a huge ancient tortoise across a tropical
sand beach.
It is hot.
I am so small compared to the turtle.
Where are we going?
Where is he taking me?

*

On my way to the Junkyards—this is not a dream—I detour to
the ArtFields.
Because of Marianna's passion for art, I am driven to learn more
about it.
And this is the place.
Marianna, my Opposite.

High walls of stacked-up soup cans stand on both sides of the
entrance—a locked chain link fence.

To enter, you must prove your devotion to ZundelState, be
proficient at animal sounds, so I make sounds.

89

Then, to show my kinship with each beast, I posture to match the sound.

Arf, I yelp, and strike a doglike pose.
Moooooo—I'm down on all fours.
I am my namesake, Gulogulo the wolverine, so I freeze, then start my satanic chaching.
"CHACH CHACH CHACH!"

The fence swings open.

I see stacked-up canvases, strewn-about canvases, randomly tossed canvases, musty, faded, ripped canvases.
Twisted canvases.
Color gone.
I wander for hours, become drowsy.

*

The ground is soft, the sky faded.
New-mown hay!
That's how the air smells.
Hay bales scattered about.
The emotional dirt gives under my feet.
Irises, weed-like, pop up through mounds of mud-caked canvases—warped canvases, poppies peeking through.

As I pass water lily ponds, I smell a smell and my eyelids droop.
Drawn towards the boozy odor, I move through a patch of woods.
How long have I been here?
Blue poles slant every which way.
I traipse across a maze of red and yellow vines.
I am walking through the history of art here.
Have I ever been anywhere else?

Dizzy, I'm down on the forest floor.
Yellowish dusk turns to evening.
Fat glittery stars swirl across the thick navy night.
A siren.
Guards steam towards me.
I'm confused.
To myself, I murmur, "I'm a historian. A historian. I'm a historian.
Follow facts," then fall into a cavernous sleep.

I'm playing harmonica in a zone called Rome, singing "I dreamt I
was walking into World War Three."
I say to Marianna "Our love's gonna grow ooh-wah, ooh-wah.
Let's go play Adam and Eve."
Smiling, she says, "I'll let you be in my dreams if I can be in
yours."
I mumble, "I said that."
Who's who is confused.

Can't move, can't turn around.
Too much furniture.
Space, I need space.
I toss a canvas onto the forest floor.
Circle it, bend, bow, weave.
Squeeze an inch of Mars Black onto a piece of plastic, drip water
on top, load the drippy paint onto a big brush.
Circle the canvas, splash the runny black.
Footprints, blobs, and splatters.
Am I me or am I Marianna?

I find myself in Smilavichy Zone now, ShtetlFields.
Marianna is with me or she *is* me—I can't tell.
I smell killed fowl.
Am I a Jewish girl sheltered in a Catholic school?
Am I a painter?

I am going to Paris.
All I want is to get out of here, to paint.

Marianna/Me is from the ancestral line of Chaim Soutine, born
in Smilavichy, near Minsk.
Now I smell blood.
Could it be paint?

I won't leave you behind, Chaim.
I'll cart you along in my airy mind, then one day you'll appear in
reds and blues and blacks and streaks of white in new forms, in
juicy oils, as newly formed beasts, as fowl, as fish, as beef.
Bloodied from violence.
You shall see: animals will take over!
The golden beastly visions of the future.
The chickens!
The skates!
The herrings!

I shall starve myself to replicate the suffering.
From within and without, from Talmudists to the State.
Painting is all.
Expression will follow my genes into the future, men, women
alike, into the unimaginable times of the future where
expressiveness is all.
Or nothing.
Banned.
My paintings will live on in secret basements and hidden attics,
through revolution.
I will make sure.
There will be a girl someday, out in the bright light.
Who loves buttercups and lives in the color yellow.
She picks them during wartime and runs a bouquet home to her
mother.

She will reign.
No, she will be stifled, but will not succumb to the State's forces,
as I have not.
It's DNA.
Is she me?
Am I Chaim?
We are one, it seems.

Dream genes confused.
Once dreams were outlawed, they became recessive.
Still an unbroken thread into the future from the far past.
That's how characteristics get passed down.

I buy my agitated oils with milk and honey money, then go
hungry to fortify my vision.

Mounds of food at the butcher.
The hanging carcasses, rolled loins, the flayed steaks.
"I want that food!"
Beautiful flesh!
Meat.
Back in my painting room, I could eat my oils.
I spend a long while laying out the tubes in rows.
Thinking about crimsons, cadmiums, pthalo blues, fish, fowl, beef.
My dreams torpedo across the studio.

Off to the slaughterhouse to buy a bloody carcass.

With paint, you can build everything.
Not a representation of a thing, but *das Ding an Sich, the thing
itself.*
The bloody carcass, the smelly fowl, the enticing herring.
When I wrestle the Rayfish to the ground, I start to wake up.

I thought I was awake!
Uh-oh, danger—merge of dream and wake, enticement of paint.
Dream-like confusion or dream?
For this woozy time, I begin to understand Marianna and her
drive.
I understand the State and its rules, its laws.
Art is dangerous.
You have nothing to lose.
Your vigor to make dominates.

And me, Joe Gulogulo?
I drive for the facts that got us here.

&&&
Kern

Even now, there are people who possess shards of the past, bits
and pieces of history that never vanished into the ether.

Marianna's ancestors were painters.
Chaim Soutine, Celia Kaplow, both from the shtetls of Minsk.
She came to learn this because during one of Joe's forays to the
Junkyards, he ended up in the ShtetlFields.

It is hard to fathom how their ancestral lines came up as a subject
to explore between them.
Each was descended from Albert Einstein, a scientist and violinist
who made many discoveries long ago.
That they both knew this was uncanny.
That they learned this fact about each other within weeks of
having met is more uncanny.

Once Joe realized they both carried Einstein's genes, he began to
wonder how closely related he and Marianna were.
Where did his passion for history come from?
Where did her passion for art come from?
Did these two things somehow intersect in the double helix?

It occurred to him that the answer might lie in the stars.
Or the birds.
Or the stars and birds.
Stardust.

Los pajaritos abandonaron el nido.
The birdies have flown the nest.

*

There's nothing new under the sun.
It turns out that time is fungible.
Not like a timeline that starts 40,000 years ago or more and
stretches straight and level across a long wall up to the present.
It exists all at once, in space.
Everything that ever happened is out there in the boundlessness
and will return again.
Nothing new will happen and nothing will be lost.
We will live again over and over.

&&&
Joe

How did I fall for Marianna?
How many times has this happened?
She was a State Worker in ShitHistory/HistoryShit Sector.

I had been brought in for questioning, as usual.
As I was waiting, this beautiful woman—my neighbor!—walked
up to me, touched my arm, and walked away.
Was she my Opposite?
It was as if she wanted to touch history.
A few days later, she appeared at my house.
Thus began our two days of nonstop talking.

"Marianna!
You are you and I am I!
Opposites, but you are my twin.
My indivisible me/you.
We are fused.
We've traveled opposing routes.
I fight with the State, and you, a ZundelState adherent, excel.
But take heed!
I am your protector from now on.
I was Soutine for a dream-filled night, wandering the ArtFields
and the ShtetlFields, and found the thread of you.
You are a maker.
You put things out.
I am a learner.
I take things in.
In out in out like breath.
The two of us, fused.

*

Marianna, I am scared to tell you what I want to tell you but I'm
more scared not to."

"Now you're scaring me."

"Why I almost trust you is, I don't know, it's weird.
You—the model ZundelState citizen, while I'm a skulking history
seeker.
Opposites!
But the whiff of you counts for everything.
It's ancestral."

"Stop.
Please stop.
Joe, you are making my blood curdle!
And there's a snake out there, barely visible.
I saw it from the corner of my eye.
I feel that the viper is either what is making our talk happen or
the other way around.
I can't tell which.
Either way, it is potent and huge.
See it?
It's slithering near that big boulder!"

"Marianna, calm down.
It's a shadow, I think.
Now, lean, lean against this rock.
Feel its warmth seep into your back.
It will help.
Skin.
Smooth skin.
Help us both.

Marianna, this—what I'm going to tell you—has been happening
at night since I was a child."

"A child? Since you were a child?"

"Yes. And I don't know why but I have always known not to tell
anyone about my night journeys.
But you, you open something inside me that stirs this all up.
A tribal draw."

"What is a tribal draw?
What are you talking about?"

"OK OK OK.
Here's what happens to me most nights.
I go to sleep and then I undergo things."

"Things?"

"Things happen.
Like last night: My muscles softened as I fell asleep.
My insides melted in the drayish dark.

"Then, Marianna, it was you, pictures of you all the time.
You are a girl running around like crazy.
Your hair is in two bunches secured by rubber bands.
We kick each other, then we both laugh.
It's uproarious!
I buy you a torch.
You become a soldier!
I put on a helmet.
Art, art! you scream.
I throw you onto the floor yelling Groinka!
Women surround us.

I yell, Soutine!
The Ukraine.
Our ancestors.

"It's exciting and wild and lively.
Smoke fills the room.
I make my way to the door, bolt outside.
Marianna, where are you?
The ground is steaming.
Glaciers are melting.
Air is unbreathable.
I'm looking everywhere for you.

"Then I wake up and the room looks like before I fell asleep, as if
nothing has happened.

"Other nights, it's other things.
Completely unpredictable.
Always makes me feel feelings and think new thoughts.
No one has ever told me anything like this happens to them.
And now I've told you.
Broken something open that can't be stuffed back inside."

&&&
Kern

As Marianna was putting together what Joe said, she kept quiet.
She steeled herself against him.
Any softness towards him she shot down.
She used every bit of her ZundelState training to fight her
hysteria.
And hysteria it was.
She took deep breaths.
She focused on one object, a low stool.
Eventually, she was able to joke with Joe.
She didn't exactly make fun of his admission, but she tried to close
the door on any conversation about it.
"Joe, you are some clown! This sounds like a thousand years in the
future! Ha! You are funny."

Marianna knew what Joe was describing.
She was somewhat horrified.

2/ Brain-O-Mat

&&&
Joe

When I enter the Brain-O-Mat, I wander, then find myself in its outer reaches.
The place that only a few are permitted to enter.
Why me, I wonder.
Is it due to the fact that I have Marianna's trust—Marianna, a loyal worker for ZundelState?

Now I'm in the deepest room of the Brain-O-Mat, looking for the big table with the long drawer full of slices of Albert Einstein's brain.
He was an inventor in the 1900s.

If you lick a slice of his brain, depending on which slice, things happen.
You might crave a doughnut.
You might smell Nagasaki after the bomb.
You might invent a refrigerator.
You might fall to your knees and pray.
You might think the mushroom cloud created the first doughnut.

It's no accident that the Brain-O-Mat is next to the Doughnut Museum, attached by an underground passageway.

Why is it taking centuries, a sign in the museum asks, *to uncover the relation between doughnuts and Albert Einstein?*
The answer—still unknown.
The riddle inspires me.

I lick a sliver.
I taste a doughnut.
Like a forest fire abruptly lit, nothing now can stop me from
intense licking.
Not the specter of the Inquisition ZundelState.
Not even pleas from Marianna, my first, my love.
Where is she?
She was right next to me a second ago, pleading with me to
upchuck the brain spittle.

That night, a brain movie floods me.
Me and another bloke are driving across a stretch of land called
America, from one end to the other, with the scientist's brain in
the trunk of our car.
There are roads.

Now I am transporting his brain across Indiana, across Missouri,
across Nebraska.
Flesh packed in formaldehyde.
Meanings subsumed beneath the thing itself.
What is the meaning of this flesh?

Einstein with his discovery and result.
Walking up the stairs.
Eating a yeast-raised doughnut.
Chewing a bite, spitting it out, testing for the proper consistency.

There is no straight line between things.
It's all a human fabrication to make sense.
Call it history if you want.
Or call it fiction.

&&&
Kern

Almost a thousand years ago, Albert Einstein dreamt he was
sledding down a steep hill.
Sledding faster and faster, he almost reached the speed of light.
The stars looked altered.
His Theory of Relativity emerged from this dreamt observation
which changed our understanding of the physical world.

One day Einstein was walking along a beach on a Long Island,
reciting Federico Garcia Lorca's poem
Verde que te quiero verde.
He felt as if he were sleepwalking.
A somnambulist.
Green wind. Green branches.
The ship out on the sea and the horse on the mountain.
He saw a future world where dreams were extinct.
History outlawed.
Art banished.

What if there was no music?
He got scared, more scared than he had ever been.
The day before, he had sailed his boat *Tinef* (*junk* in that dead
language Yiddish) out from Horseshoe Cove to collect his mail.
Later, he stood on his porch playing his violin.
What if no violins?

He felt fear in his bones.
Later that summer he wrote to President Franklin Delano
Roosevelt, warning him of "extremely powerful bombs of a new
type."

The letter, a spur to the invention of the atomic bomb, employed Einstein's Theory of Relativity.
Einstein was haunted that his brain indirectly invented the bomb.

But as he peered ahead into the ball of time, he saw worse threats.
Time, that infinitely folding thing.
The mind, that conundrum.
Dreams, gold.
What if they disappeared?

During Einstein's lifetime, people possessed a thing called the unconscious.
Your unconscious could drive you around any bend and you'd barely realize it.
Dreams were the jewels of the unconscious.

Einstein's schoolteachers in his boyhood town Ulm labeled him *vertraumt*, meaning *dreamy*.

Once Einstein dreamt of fields of wheat and millstones.
"Flour!" he woke up exclaiming.
And so began his creating the first doughnut.
It was like a cushion and fluffy.
Its inside was jelly.
When a person ate one, they felt better.
More better than you would think.
Out of proportion to what the doughnut was.

It's about eating dough and the comfort that provides.

&&&
Joe

As I fell asleep in the spectral dark,
my shore began sloshing against the sides of me,
moistening my rough-cut mind.

I see the mushroom cloud above Hiroshima.
I walk into a museum room filled with containers of human flesh
suspended in liquid.

I watch the little scientist walk up a staircase in a wooden house
on a Long Island.
He enters a kitchen, sits at a table, eats a yeast-raised doughnut.
He chews a bite, spits it out, testing, testing.
He is inventing doughnuts.
Lots of Japanese people are dead.
He wants to comfort them.

I am watching a short man named Albert walking slowly, looking
at every leaf and bug and cloud.
He's in a little beach town.
Now he's in a hardware store looking at every brand of deep fryer.
Now he's tucking one into the backseat of his old car.
Now he wanders into a food store, reads every word on each food
label of cooking oil and flour.
He looks pleased!

For years he has been eating dough to assuage his tragic dose of
life, he, Albert, the pacifist.

Eating dough.
Finding the right small bowl in the cupboard, butter, flour, and a
pinch of sugar, only a pinch, blended with finger or fork and then
consumed.
No comfort like dough.
Sweet possibility, texture of cloud, surround of goodness.

He experimented with yeast, with no yeast, by kneading, by
fermenting the dough, by injecting grape jam after frying, warm
rooms for the dough to rise faster, cold rooms for the dough to
rise slow, this oil, that oil, this pan, that pan, this jam, that jam.

I am eating dough.
I see a mushroom cloud.
I am eating a mushroom pizza.
I see burned everything.
People. Pizza.
Dead. Mangled.
Millions of them.
Energy unleashed.
Unleashed by me.
I am not dead.
I am a raging Jewish stream of guilt overflowing every bank.
Imprisoned.
Maybe doughnuts will assuage the pain.
A comfort shop on every Japanese corner.

*

Next night I fall to sleep, my shore sloshing against me, waves
breaking over my mind.

What is happening?
Now I see the mushroom cloud hanging over Hiroshima.
The Inquisition.

The smell of frying dough from every Jewish household.
A clue.
I need comfort for myself.

I am wandering through a flaming barbecue forest.
No hands.
No legs.
Eyes blue, bright and wide open.
Smart eyes.
My mind, rampant and wild.
Frogs, frog legs.
Mushrooms!
Insane fungal ignition!
History melts into one bitter, blasted mushroom boat.

*

Speaking of history, a few hundred years after doughnut shops
dominated the Japanese lands, they began to appear throughout
space.
3D printing had taken over food production, Earthlings traveling
to the outer reaches of the Milky Way could print out their meals.
Spaceships carried edible inks on their journeys.
When they landed on exoplanet Kepler-22b, the Earth travelers
printed doughnuts, a gift for the inhabitants, who loved them.
Earlier humans had decided not to print jelly doughnuts, then
changed their minds.
This led to unexpected outcomes.
Jelly doughnuts!
The Moloko Plus Jelly was magic!

I found this strange item at the bottom of a Junkyard carton. DCA stood for Doughnut Corporation of America, I do believe.

3/ DNA

&&&
Joe

Reader, I have a huge appetite—jelly doughnuts, frog legs,
mushroom pizzas, barbecued meat of any type.
I especially love berries and eggs.
The scientific name of the wolverine—gulo gulo—comes from the
Latin word *gulo*, meaning *glutton*.

This is because, as well as having a ferocious temper, the wolverine
has a ferocious appetite.
When it eats, it eats quickly and voraciously, leaving nothing
behind, almost as if it hadn't eaten in days, or as if it will never eat
again.

According to scientists, this habit may be the result of the scarcity
of food in the wolverine's habitat.
It will eat just about anything: deer, porcupines, beavers, squirrels,
foxes, rabbits, voles, lemmings, mice, birds, birds' eggs, and if it has
to, even berries.
I consume history with the same ferociousness.
My name was given to me because of my gluttony for facts.
The scarcity of historical facts in my habitat feeds this gluttony.

*

A siren.
Guards steaming towards me.
Confused, I yell "But I'm a historian.
I am a historian!"

The Guards circle me, confer.

They scare me.
One day they will harm me, but I will never know which day.

I used to hate the past, hated history.
Now I'm obsessed by it.
History got me by the balls.
It was a gradual comeuppance, so to speak.

ZundelState prohibits the study of history.
Zundel, the ancient sage who denied history, father to the State.

Entrance to the Junkyards is forbidden.
But I have access to the Junkyards, via a unique, albeit fake,
passport.
A convoluted story I might tell you later.

On one sojourn to the Junkyards, I secured a cardboard carton full
of ancient pamphlets from a place called Los Alamos.
In the box was a hand-scrawled note on a napkin that said
"A. Einstein."
Puzzling.

From the Introduction to the first pamphlet:
*One of the chief difficulties in securing data for this volume arose from
security restrictions during the early operations of the Project.*
*Many of the transactions were carried on orally to ensure secrecy, and
so no "written" record was preserved.*
In other instances, data were destroyed to further protect the secret.
*This complete secrecy was one of the most amazing aspects of the entire
program, but it produced one of the greatest obstacles to piecing the story
together for historical purposes.*

Piecing stories together for historical purposes—the central force of
my life.
I am on a quest to discover ZundelState's secret.

And I have a personal secret.

The secrets are related.

During many nights, I suspect I live in a realm not shared by others.

All related.

You see, Reader, from the time I was a child, I have always watched nighttime brain movies.

Not "watch."

Feel. I feel them.

I think they are *dreams.*

I think that's what dreams were.

I always knew to keep this hidden until I met Marianna.

I once did tell her about it and she acted odd.

I sometimes wonder, why was I chosen to fill my nights this way?

*

Here's an essay I found in a Junkyard box.

In twentieth-century America, people studied dreaming, which William Stafford, a great dreamer, described.

Improving Your Dreams

The way you are supposed to dream is this—you study the dreams of others, especially of those who have succeeded, those whose dreams have met the test of time. You extract from successful dreams the elements that work. Then you carefully fashion dreams of your own. This way you can be sure to have admirable dreams, ones that will appeal to the educated public.

As your technique improves, you will find your dreams accepted more and more: what doesn't work, you learn to leave out.

Of course, now and then (you won't be able to help it) some strange, untried elements will creep into your dreams- you can't be careful and responsible all the time. And of those stray flaws, a few may be good luck, and you will keep them; they are signs of some rules not yet discovered. And if you are scholarly you may save up an account of them, and later offer the account to apprentices so that they may dream properly.

Thus, over generations, the quality of dreams will improve; a tradition will accumulate, with skills and crafts that can be passed along.

Ambitious and reliable people can study about dreaming and then become worthy of dreaming themselves. If they start a weak dream, one with clichés or irregularities, or if they let themselves wander into an unstructured dream that violates the best in the tradition, they can stop themselves and hold staunchly to standards.

Quality is achieved by cleaving to those standards. As one respected critic has said, "Every time you accept an unworthy dream, you are damaging the tradition of American dreaming."

Problems with this approach abounded.
Once students learned to perfect dreams, eventually all dreams were more or less the same.
As time went on, there was no reason to dream.
Once Animoxins took over the state, dreams were outlawed.
Areas of the brain that produced dreams disappeared, the same way toes, tailbones, and the appendix did.

Secondarily, a small form of literature called *poetry* disappeared somewhat for the same reason.
Although poets were rare, they too had schools to improve their poems.
Once there were perfect poems, the section of the brain that created them (akin to the dream-making area) vanished.

*

I am touching Marianna's back.
She is bending over to pick something up from the street.

Now I am touching her arm.
Some kind of charm.

When she told me her secret, we were high up on a rock-strewn
hill overlooking a pink city.
The air was so warm.
Her face was soft.
Her black eyes shining, her forehead clear.
"I know the secret."
Then, like an erupting volcano, she spewed her lava out.

Dreams!
People had them every night!
They led the way!
They filled longing!
They created longing.
Full of make-believe or not.
Their effect, monumental.
Their stretch, dimensionless.

Dreams came to Marianna only a few times—each florid and each
feeding her love of art.
What is *pthalo blue*?
What is *horsehair brush*?

I dreamed from the start, all historical.
FDR's grocery list.
Crimean War.
Einstein's sandals.

Our first meeting was chemically fiery and felt familial.
Sibling lust arose from dreaming.

Marianna, you are my love.
I hate you.

You are my mirror.
The wispiness of your hair, the way you set your chin,
your shyness, your courage.
Ay! Is it all a dream.
Is to dream to love?
Is to love to dream?
I am riddled with confusion.

&&&
Marianna

Joe, last night was summer and so muggy.
Sleep settled on me like a light blanket.
The bed—piercingly luxe.
Distant party music as I was falling asleep.

Pictures filled my brain.
The dead walk across my screen.
This dead one.
That dead one.
My long-gone father waves.
He's in a canoe dismantling a beaver house.
He's gliding down a hill on skis.
Strangely, in sleep I know what beavers are, I know what skis are.
I hear my dead mother's dead friend ebulliently laughing.

I rush upstairs spiraling to a steeple.
Height so terrifying I get paralyzed.
Can't go down.
Can't turn around.
Fixed, I can't move.
Doves fly outside.
Bells chime.
Crowds are gathering.
Horns wail.
Death abounds.
The wind stops.
Horns go silent.
The crowd evaporates.

A fetid odor invades.
Sheets pile up.

Drumming.
Oh it's winter now.
I look for farina.
Hot, white comfort.
When I find it, it's too bright.
My eyes go blind.
My hands go limp.
My nose bleeds.
Blood flowing out of my vagina.

&&&
Kern

"Joe. I want tongue."

Joe and Marianna were celebrating Marianna's birthday at a fancy restaurant.
Tongue was hard to come by, but they served it at this new place that had opened up right under the Bridge.
All the tables viewed the Water, and the views were spacious and full of motion—at least twenty fans on the ceiling of each room silently moving the hot air.

When Marianna ordered tongue, her anticipation got the better of her.
How would it arrive?
Her anxiety mounted.
An image rose in her mind like a flag flapping—hands of women cut off at the wrist grilled on a barbecue, a sizzling delicacy.
Her mind jumped to a friend who had traveled to the banks of Asia River and as he approached the burning bodies, he got sick, overwhelmed by the smell.
The smell was not bad, it was good, and that was the rub.

"I want to be human," she thought.
"You are what you eat," she thought.
Nothing calmed her down.
She counted.
By ones—no good.
She thought of Popeye saying "I yam what I yam."
By twos—2 ... 4 ... 6 ... 8 ..., no good.
Had to be harder to occupy her racing mind.

Threes might work—3 ... 6 ... 9 ... 12 ....
Better.

Her food had already arrived.
Tongue in sauce.
A waiter came over with a hunk of horseradish big as a baby's arm
and shaved thin slices of it onto the edge of the plate.
She savored each bite, filled to the brim with the intriguing
texture of tongue.

There was an odd air of festivity as when, centuries earlier, Marco
Polo visited the Court of Kublai Khan and watched as a lion,
unchained, lay motionless and subservient at Kublai Khan's feet as
he ate.

There was an electricity to the spot, the restaurant vertical and
brick.
Five floors looked out to the Water—each specialized in a dish.
The Hunt Room—hare and venison.
The Quiet Room served tongue.
A throwback to old Japanese delicacies was the Boletus Room—
chanterelles, morels, and boleti served in every type of sauce.
One floor served brain.
Photos of Albert Einstein, the scientist, decorated the room.
Tupperware containers of formaldehyde in glass display cases
lined one wall.
There were arguments whether to name the room the Brain Trust
or the Brain Drain.
The Egg Room occupied the top floor.
It was impossible to gain entry.
A sign on the locked door read: *An egg is the most private thing in
the world until it is broken.*

At the birthday dinner in the Quiet Room, Joe informed
Marianna he was going to lick every sliver of Einstein's brain at

the Brain-O-Mat until the light of history flashed on.
She pointed out how he became violent when he licked some slivers, just like Einstein as a child.
How he threw chairs at people.
Or hit them with a pickaxe just as Einstein did to his sister.
She questioned his quest, to no avail.

*

When Joe made his thirty-eighth trip to the Brain-O-Mat, he licked a brain sliver.
Pop.
He saw this.

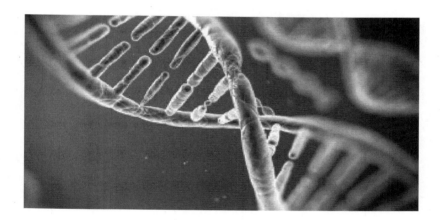

Progress.

*

Joe and Marianna shared Albert Einstein's dream gene as did all of his descendants.
Some dominant.
Some recessive.
Written into the gene was secrecy as well as dreaminess.
And so Joe dreamed.

&&&
Joe

High up here, the air is tinged with disappearance.
I make a nest of soft pine needles.
Plush comfort to the vision of poison mushroom clouds.

REM sleep is now doughy.
Now doughnutty.

Cold air, snowflakes spiraling in the black night, lit by fiery
torches.
Grape jelly.
Soufganiot.
A dancing black-hatted man hands me a jelly doughnut.

All I want is to watch early-morning birds fly when I awake from
a night full of dreaming, gathering strength from watching.
Songbirds, crows, snow geese—they are flying in odd groupings
now.
Is this dreaming or happening now in the daybreak sky?
Strength is what I need to understand this blur of dream and real.

I need to muster vigor to grasp my Junkyard findings.
When I unpack my Junkyard carton of Los Alamos maps, there
are shapes and lines, numbers and labels.

I stand and proclaim:

Omega Site
South Mesa Site
Beta Site

Two-Mile Mesa South Site
Anchor West Site
Anchor East Site
K-Site
Q-Site
R-Site
S-Site
Pajarito Laboratory

I was startled.
I got scared.
Bad nerves blanketed me.
My legs turned to jelly.
My breath quickened.
Onward I read.

DP-Site
TD-Site
Magazine Area A
Ten Site
Kappa Site
Ancho Canyon Site
Frijoles Mesa Site
Waste Management Site
Fenton Hill Site
PF-Site
OH-Site
East Jemez Site
Pajarito Service Site

Pajarito—Oh no, not again.

Central Guard Site
Central Tech Support Site
Water Canyon Site

Anchor North Site
Rio Grande Site
Airport Site
Pajarito Mesa Site

Pajarito Mesa Site
Los pajaritos abandonaron el nido.
The birdies have flown the nest.
Birdies are dreams.
Nest, the brain.

The day the atomic bomb dropped on Nagasaki began the
beginning of the end of dreaming.
No one knew until centuries later.
The birdies had flown the nest.

&&&
Kern

Albert Einstein foresaw that future worlds would
obliterate dreaming.
So he concocted a formula—his dream genes would live on
in his descendants.
He created a genetic pathway for the return of dreams.
Thus, a few humans heavily sauced with his genes never stopped
dreaming and never revealed it to anyone.
Not until Joe and Marianna fell into love.
Love is stronger than secrets.
Dreams more potent than love.

Much was recorded about Einstein's discovery of relativity, much
about his work on the Japanese doughnut shops, but zero about
the gene for dreaming that he passed on to his descendants.
It was his secret from the world, his successful attempt to prolong
humanness in humans.

Scholars have argued over Einstein's discoveries: the theory of
relativity led to the bomb, which led to the invention of comfort,
provided through Japanese doughnut shops.
ZundelState forbids the exploration to discover how Einstein's
*gene*ius passed down his vertraumtness, his dreaminess.

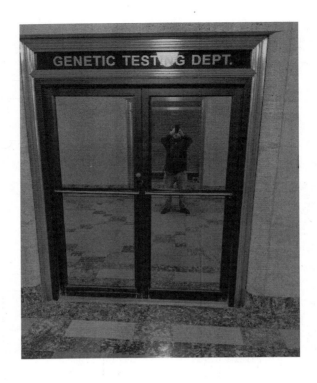

When Joe arrived home from the Junkyard Zones, he carried a box into his house, set it on the floor, and sat next to it.
A faint roar that he could not identify came from the box.
It soothed him.
Whoooosshhh ... Pause ... Whoooooosshh ... Pause ...
His rosy cheeks moistened.
Joe began to sway back and forth.
The sight of the double helix he had seen at the Brain-O-Mat lodged itself inside his brain.

Dusk was settling on the hills.
Two black crows flew across the peachy sky.
The waning moon slipped from view.
Joe *relaxed*, that was the word for this.
He moved slowly as he set the object called *shell* on the floor and

looked closely.
It was a perfect double.
He fingered it.

He stretched his long form on the floor, shut his eyes, and fell asleep into a vast sea of pleasure.

Joe found himself in a small orange rubber boat that he could power himself.
Whooosshh … Pause … Whoooshhh … Pause …
He was skimming across a large wet area—huge swells of water made the boat ride up and down, a motion Joe had never known. Was this *lullabye?*

Bye bye.
The boat was crossing water.
Joe was guiding it.
He saw an island, headed over the waves towards it as the sky turned from dark to light.
On the shore were silhouettes of jagged mountains, which fell straight down to the shore—only a shred of beach between their base and the sea.

Fresh air blew over his cheeks.
He headed towards his island of deep sleep.
Joe's breathing became larger and stronger—in, out, in, out.
Joe was inhaling new air, expelling old.
His lungs inflated like a giant's bellows.

He bit his lip and startled, awoke.
He moved his long torso and legs, and sat up, looked outside.
By now the full sun had risen clear.
The tops of the trees had an orange hue.
Joe walked around the room, lay back down on the floor, and
within a few minutes, he slept again.

In, out, in, out—his strong solid breath lulled him back onto the
beach.
Sand!
He sank his hands into it, and it was warm and granular.
He would never feel poison on them again.
He took off his shoes.
His lungs took in delicious air and expanded, so that Joe gained
zest.
The world was large.
The world was quiet.

Joe lay down in the sand and it warmed him.
He gazed up at the clear sky and began to fall asleep.
In his sleep, he slept again, a double dose.
He passed through portholes.
In his sleep, he shifted his grand weight in the sand.
His elbow felt something and he reached his lanky arm towards it.
He outstretched his arm, unbent his elbow, curled his fingers
around the object.
It was the twin of the object he found in the box.
As if he were caressing his own body, he caressed the object.

He awoke from this double sleep and sat up in the sand, his hands wrapped around the object.
There were others on the beach.
Each was different.
Each suggested mysteries and answers.
He stood up and walked to the left, where the land veered down towards what looked like a streambed.
He came upon something that looked like a cross between a fish skeleton and a snake skeleton.
Never had he seen such uncorrupted bleached white.
Was this the color of time?

If gentleness can be violent, his was.
It woke him.
There he was, adrift on the floor.

*

Verboten—his heart was saying that word to him by way of rhythm.
Ver boten, ver boten—bum bumbum bum bumbum bum bumbum—his heart spoke to him through its beat.
His heart took the place of talk.
It was like a mother.

The heart's beat is direct—goes straight from heart to brain — when it speaks, Joe has a guide through the world with all its frailties.
One time his heart went like this: ba bum ba bum bumbum—again—ba bum ba bum bumbum.
What on earth was his heart telling him, it was hard to decipher.
And then he knew.
I want my real mama. I want my real mama.

Then it beat this way.
Ba bum ba bumbum? Ba bum ba bumbum?
And he not only figured it out, something in him *remembered*
those words.
Remember—what might that have meant?
What could it have meant?
And why on earth would those words matter to Joe Gulogulo.

All at once, *Are you my mother?* rose to the surface
of his rippling mind.
His mind now a large sea.
Surfer waves crashed upon the shore in time, in rhythm.
Whooooooshhh … Pause … Whoooshhh … Pause …
That phrase floated atop the waves' crests.
Float and repeat.
Float and repeat.

Is the ocean my mother?
Maybe that's the key, the code to break.
Joe was haunted.
His need to dry off and settle himself solidly on dry land
was strong.
The waves subsided, but the sound remained.

*

In the early 2100s, people stopped reporting their dreams
to each other.
Dreams riled up possibility and made for questioning.

Ancient ZundelState was threatened by the effects
of people dreaming.
They announced a simple explanation to gradually delete dreams
from existence.
Dreams inspired bad inventions like the annihilating bomb.

One traveled too far afield in dreams. Dreams were related to "imagination," a concept we know almost nothing about today, but it was bad for society.

In the olden days, people used to report their dreams to each other many mornings.
But that tradition was abandoned hundreds of years ago.
Joe knew about this from a teenage girl's journal he had procured on a Junkyard history trip:

Windows open, no breeze. Hot night. Finally fell asleep about 3 only to wake at 6, started downstairs and saw Nonna and Aunt Jo eating soft-boiled eggs at the kitchen table. I sat on the stairs listening as they told each other their dreams in the still morning air. Jo began.
"Some man walked towards me. He was shirtless—what a beautiful chest!—and sweaty. Shiny. My legs turned jelly-like and my knees gave out. Then I fell and was crawling in the unmowed grass towards the rose bed. Then, it must have been his brother, got out of an old green car. Slicked black hair, he tried to hand me a box of cracker-jacks. I couldn't hold it. I waved or something and kept crawling."
Then Nonna. "Oh Jo! I dreamt I was in a cold place. Maybe it was Greenland. It was a short, simple dream. There were icebergs! I kept climbing up one and sliding down into the water. It was freezing and slippery but there was a cotton candy stand at the top. It's so hot today!"
They put up another pot of fresh coffee, opened the box of doughnuts, and continued their dream talk. I got dressed, went out, and walked along the purple iris patch. I couldn't remember any dreams from last night but I'm pretty sure I had scary ones. I'm forgetting my dreams more and more.

4/ DuoDreaming

&&&
Kern

It's a few hundred years *after* Nonna and Aunt Jo.
People, upon waking, report on their night's sleep like this.
"I slept well last night. My screen was dark black."
Or, "Last night so little sleep, light grey, everything light grey."
It was as if there was a blank screen, which varied from shades of
light grey to dark black.
As if something might appear on the screen but never would.

This is what it's like not to dream.
Nothing is what it's like.
No fancy flights, no scary heights, no slanty buildings, no sex.
No cute dark-haired guy saying, "I like your tits."
No nothing.

A grey screen.
A black screen.
A white one.

*

A man named Pavel, an Einstein descendant, takes his shoes off.
This is a few hundred years before Joe and Marianna.
The dirt path in the forest feels like part of him.
Wind, dirt, and Pavel are one.
He loves to run.
Each day when he does, he counts the birds.
Pavel's mind is feather-like, his body lanky.
His yearning is palpable to the birds.
Dreambirds populate his heart, fluttery wings adrift.

139

The sound—wave of wing or brush on a drum?
Like a hummingbird, his heart is constantly moving.

Birdheart.
Featherheart.
Dreamheart.
Los pajaritos abandonaron el nido.
The birdies have flown the nest.
What am I made from?—the question plagues Pavel.

Birds in flight become thought-like and men's thinking resembles flight.
Pavel muses on Einstein's ancient premise.
With a hefty dose of his DNA, Pavel descends from the scientist,
thus he's always been a profuse and secret dreamer.

*

He slows down, sits on the ground, leans against the khaki
umbrella tree.
"I am not hearing bird song."
"My legs are giving out."

His heart seeks dreambirds,
fluttering wings breathe,
weight adrift moving through.
What is happening to my body?
He is terrified.

A black feather in the brush.
A startled crow.
Ahh, ahh, ahh.
Ahhh, ahh, ahh.

Dreams alight like feathers, the heart's wings.
It is the season when light slants between trees.

His heart is beating.
The sun pours yellow in the woods.

Crows pick at Pavel's teeth while he sleeps.
Then, sounding a warning, they caw back and forth.
Pavel is afraid of snakes and so are the crows.
The crows are trying to scare the snakes from Pavel's back barn,
where they slither around with hunted remains piled high.
Piles of bones.
An awful cawing wakens him.
The crows' sound alerts him, calls him to his mission.

Passing down his genetic material is the only hope for humankind.
He feels the weight.
He understands how much depends on his vertraumt genes.
He wants to uphold his end of the human bargain.
Dwindling birds in the empty field, messengers.
If he could just sit by the water at the ocean beach and daydream,
but no.
To himself, he says "Save dreams, you fucking motherfucker fuck!"

*

One night long, long ago—Albert Einstein's century—a geneticist
named James Watson had a dream in which he saw two snakes
twisted around each other with their heads at opposite ends.
His discovery of the double helix—the structure of DNA—grew
from this dream.
Dreams were still abundant when Watson dreamt his snake
dream.

Reader, can you see that big white bird in the distance?
Just look.
It is fixated on the runner, Pavel, although that is beyond your
vision.

Pavel nestles into the mesh of leaves, lies down.
The white bird does not avert its eyes.
Pavel closes his, dozes.
A dream floats through.
The wind picks up, blows leaves around his body.
Everything is soft and floaty.
His corporeal self is all there.

Flocks of snow geese fill the sky, pumping their large wings
through the clouds, the screen of blue sky locked.

*

Pavel dreams as the fat white bird watches:

My mother!
My plump mother, humming Chopin's nocturnes in our kitchen.
She's young, she's old!
My luftmensch father with pencil and paper making equations,
murmuring "The Jew. Einstein the Jew."
Crash!
The cash register rings "Kaching!"
Boom!
Golems march through!
A waterfall of blood!

Pavel has fallen down a well in the cold rain, playing word games
with Albert Einstein, who is murmuring:
Doughnuts
Dreams
Nagasaki
Genes

Morning comes and the hoopoe bird accompanies Pavel on his
woodland run.
He stops to watch the enchanting birds singing.
Dreams are the sap that runs through time.

*

Many people in society were beginning to grasp the priceless value
of dreams.
Dreams were auctioned off.
In cities, crowds of wealthy people gathered in oversized rooms
with monstrous high ceilings and painful acoustics cheering loud-
mouthed auctioneers.
Everything was loud and big, and there was no room to breathe.

"How much will it be for the Empire State Building?
A dream of architectural beauty.
Corridors, lights, ceilings, preserved as cream.
Soon to evaporate.
One mil, now two mil, ha! now up to five mil, five million, five
million, going, going, gone!"
After all the good dreams were auctioned off, wealthy people
began to vie for nightmares.

"A walk in ancient New York City, how much will this old mare
go for?" the auctioneer screeched.
Buildings slant down, slam into your face.
They aren't just too big, they awkwardly chunk out to the side,
obliterating the sky.
Instead of windows, instead of billboards, it feels like
monumentally sized words slash at your face.
SHAZAM!
The word covers a quarter-mile side of a building.

Your brain contracts.
No space.
No room to have one measly thought of your own.

Pavel had traveled to the auction out of perverse curiosity.
There wasn't one bird left in this place.
No chirping.
Nothing taking flight.
No flutter of wings.
Nothing light.
Day turned to night.

Fear of late-night dark, Pavel had to get out of there.
And here he is, sitting on the pavement, wishing for dirt, looking at his feet.
Thinking of the shamanic wind, the shamanic water.
Cars far away and people too.
How to get out of here?
Nothing to do but wait.

Pavel wanders around the river's shore in the purple dark.
Dreaming there has slowed almost to a dead stop, sputtering out.
He's pondering the noise, the size of things.
He's scared shitless that dreams will totally disappear.

He thinks about art.
How scrappy.
He reaches back in his mind to the sound of Chopin's nocturnes.
Is there anything to comprehend here?
Yes, yellow.
Fields of yellow mustard.
Torrential rains.
To himself, Pavel says, "There is not one bird left in this town."
Not a single pajarito.

*

Pavel walks into Grand Central Station, his dream that will evaporate soon.

The sound of a minuet.
A formal dance.
Pavel approaches an ageless, beautiful woman.
Her hair is long and white, her limbs supple.
As they approach one another, each extends a hand.
The notes resound.
The minuet proceeds.

She says his name.
Pavel.
He corrects her—*Pa*vel, stress on the first syllable.
She says, "You just walked onto my pages."
He says, "That is as it should be."

He begins to cry, understanding that this dream is about to vanish.
His face is covered in tears.
Has he waited too long?
The minuet proceeds.
They each sit on a formal chair from centuries earlier, facing one another.
She is stoic.
He is beside himself.
The music is reverberating in his head as he weeps.

Suddenly a cello is playing deep, long-drawn-out notes, a different kind of minuet.

*

Time has collapsed, become elastic.
What has been will be again, what has been done will be done again; there is nothing new under the sun.
It is summertime, centuries before the birth of Jesus.
People think the earth is flat.
Joe is sitting on the dirt floor in a limestone cave of the Agora in a land called Athens.
Another man is there too.
Joe is pulling books from a carton. They are all thin, some bluish and others a mustardy yellow, all with the word Plato on the front.

He looks at his wrist with the bracelet with the Agora rock, his most coveted possession.

What is Plato? Why is the bracelet feeling heavy? He takes it off.

Joe knows caveness, being inside a structure, cut off from everything else in the world, on a mission for knowledge. Or is this nostalgia?
What *is* nostalgia?

He has no clue.

It is akin to how he normally felt in the presence of others in a room.

Everyone listening to the sounds of the birds flying overhead, the flapping of their grand wings, their cries—everyone, everyone focused on the third thing, the same thing.

"Los pajaritos abandonaron el nido," Joe says aloud.

The birdies have flown the nest.

"The human mind is an aviary!" exclaims the man.

With his hands, he mimes the flight of pigeons.

Now he is fixing tea.

"I'm Socrates," says the man.

He glances up to the row of vessels holding poison, says he will die the next day.

Joe wants to tell him everything he knows before it is too late.

He stupidly blurts out that centuries earlier robots and machines took over all the jobs of the State.

"Bow wow, arf arf," explains Joe.

Now experiments are being done to combine different kinds of animals, to create beasts that would alleviate problems created by the technostate.

Joe sings "One Way To Learn" to Socrates.

Take a steam bath,
smoke yourself with spruce or cedar.
Smoke your clothes too.
Go mix with the animals—
they can't smell you now.
Watch what they do.

He sings it twice, then adds, "Let's sing it as a round," and the old man joins in.

147

"Now I want to sing my song," so, in his deep alto, Socrates begins his low, slow ballad.

The earth is of vast extent, and we inhabit only a small portion of it, and dwell round the sea, like ants or frogs round a marsh.

Bending down so he doesn't hit the ceiling, Socrates stands up in the cave, continues:

The earth itself lies pure in the purity of the heavens, wherein are the stars, and which men who speak of these things commonly call ether.

The old man's big hulk starts to sway slowly.
"Have no fear," he says.
Now Socrates glances at the vessels of poison and his eyes fill with tears.

If any man could take wings and fly upward, he would look up and see a world beyond, just as the fishes look forth from the sea, and behold our world. And he would know that that was the real heaven, and the real light, and the real earth, if his nature were able to endure the sight.

The ballad is over.
The two men sit silently, both spent.

Eventually Joe begins to mumble about how ZundelState functions.
How dreams are outlawed, how expressiveness is outlawed, but how nothing can remove the forward motion to be human.
There is so much to tell the old, bearded man.

Socrates tells Joe about his friend Herodotus who wrote about the people of Atlantis—an ancient people who did not dream.
The two men discuss where those dreamless people might have gone. Hours pass.

*

In one layer of time—vertical, not horizontal time—Joe and
Socrates are conversing and singing in the Agora cave, and
simultaneously, in another layer, Marianna is making a cave in her
house.
The cave is her sanctuary, her querencia.
She has framed photos of her mama, her papa, and her brother
hanging on the wall.
There they are, almost real, almost touchable.
She imagines their long-gone voices.
She loves lying on the floor and watching the wind blow and the
snow fall.
The protection.
The quiet.
How it smells.
How the air feels.
What the low-bound light is like.
All this provides Marianna with breath.
Her cave, her home, gives her the zitzfleish, the strength, to be
an outstanding member of ZundelState, ofttimes called the
ZundelBund, her priority.
Then, in slow motion, she begins to daydream.

*

"Another day, another dollar," Marianna says to herself as she gets
ready to leave her cave and set out for work.
That is what people often say as they embark on a ZundelState
workday, but no one seems to know what on earth the phrase
means.
Just saying those words motivates people to get going.

&&&
Marianna

I love my job since I've been promoted to track the self-scales of places.
I used to track individual's self-scales, but that gave me problems.
I don't know, I'd get confused.

Wow, I just looked up and the sky is so blue.
Birds in droves, in flight.
Los pajaritos.

Wait, wait—I want to explain to you what self-scales are.
They are the greatest.
When a person is Elsewhere, meaning not concealed in their own home, there is no self.
As you know, at home, the self thinks thoughts, has passions.
The self sometimes makes things up.
That used to have a name—*imagination*.
When selves go out in the open, ZundelState is threatened.
Thus, they are eradicated when the self-scale gets too high.
The self in the Agora must never be permitted.
My job is to help with this!
It's a lot of responsibility.

It is fine to be passionate about art the way I am, as long as passion stays homebound.
I wonder if hanging my canvases on the laundry line is asking for trouble.
I don't know, I think it's fine.

What's not fine is for Joe Gulogulo to exert his passion
the way he does.
He ventures out illegally to the Junkyards to feed
his lust for history.
His goal—to learn ZundelState's secret.

The thing is: you have to keep things separate.
I'm really good at that.
Joe is not.
I'm scared for him, scared he'll get caught.
There's Home and there's Elsewhere.
That's that.

Back to self-scales.
This is how my job works.
Every day every person's quantity of self is automatically measured
on a scale from 1 to 100.
Numbers pour into my office from every town and
every person in it.
I don't understand the technology of how this works but it
actually really does.
When a town's average self-scale reaches 50, I tap my machine.
Automatically, the houses in the town dissolve.
Everyone becomes homeless.
No refuge.
It's really bad for people, but it is necessary.

Now, if the average self-scale suddenly rises above 75, I tap my
other machine, the small one, and the people in the town dissolve
as well as their houses.
This is quite rare, of course.
To be honest, I have a lot of power.

As a person, at home, you know that your self-scale is registered
daily, and that affects your life or, in some cases, time of death.

People are used to this.
You have to get used to it.

It was an important advance for ZundelState to implement this
system—towns and people dissolving, leaving no trace.
It is a clear way to upend history.
No artifacts ever to be dug up and studied for their meaning.
No bones.
No bricks.
No gold earrings.
And no cartons of books and pamphlets.
No teeth.
No pot shards.
ZundelSate's reality can never be questioned.
It just is what it is.
Anyway, I do love serving ZundelState and excelling at my job.
It's what my grandmother did and it's what I do.

&&&
Kern

A sparrow on the ground.
A peacock in a tree.
Signals of change abound.
Nights crouch in.
Stars are changing position.
The ground is wet.
The dirt is wet.
The grass is wet.
The muscle between star and earth is tightening.

Wetlands, swamps, hayfields, croplands—
the land words fly away from.
Now, high in the trees, low-swooping birds brush the hill's peak.

Los pajaritos abandonaron el nido.
The birdies have flown the nest.
Birdies are dreams.
Nest, the brain.

Masses of red birds swarm across the screen of sky.
It is spring.
Nests blown apart by winter's winds.

"Thinking is to man what flying is to birds."
Long ago, Albert Einstein enunciated these words aloud.

A breeze blows on his body, then his brain flies.
Einstein smiles to himself, remembers being in Shanghai

hilariously laughing with his wife Elsa at drinky dunking birds, a physics toy in motion.
Ha!
Life is funny!

That summer he lived on the Long Island, he befriended a pair of cardinals, observed their fidelity.
The birds cared for each other in a way he never knew.
Monogamy was foreign to him.

He talked to the birds.
"Hi, Birdie.
We're friends.
You know I'm here and I know you're here.
We're friends.
Hi, Birdie, Birdie.
Hi."

On his porch, Einstein listened to the cardinals sing, which flavored his spiraling thoughts.

When he saw the male take wing, his brain would sting with
thought.
Western wind stirred man and bird.
To the wind, to the birds, Einstein said:

> *Westron wynde, when wilt thou blow,*
> *The small raine down can raine.*
> *Cryst, if my love were in my armes*
> *And I in my bedde again*

*

Einstein loved the ladies.
By accident, when he fought dream extinction via genetics, he
also, accidentally, insured the resurgence of philandering.

Dreaming, notdreaming, philandering, notphilandering, traveling
up and down the ladder of time, all these raggedy threads are
wired and woven into earth's absurd fabric.

*

In this topmost layer of present time, in the warp and weft of
this planetary cloth, Joe Gulogulo and Marianna stumble upon
something new.

You think, Reader, there is nothing new under the sun?
Well, you are mistaken.
We all are.
There has been a change and it is called DuoDreaming.
What forces produced such a thing?
Moreover, why?
What is our earth striving towards?
Did this occur because of some genetic abnormality with
Einstein's recessive genes for dreaming and philandering?

155

God only knows.

In the wide, boundaryless world of 3090, qualities that had been recessive for centuries began to appear as dominant in more and more people.

In the midst of this world, Joe and Marianna wove their way down a new path of discovery: inhabiting a dream together, somewhat like a shared passion cave.

*

Goodnight.
Now to bed.
A genital mesh, yes.
Foreplay, yes.
But no ooohhhs, no boobs, no ahhhs, no clit, no sweat, no suck, no
asshole, no cock, no!
But ding!
Climax.
You would have to call it sexual.

*

Joe and Marianna are staying at a cabin out in the middle of the
black sand desert, not far from the Junkyards.
It is flat.
It is the place where ancient astronauts trained before traveling
beyond the Milky Way.
It is the place on Earth most like the distant lands of infinite
space.

They had gone for a walk.

"Joe, let's head back to our cabin," says Marianna.
"We can relax and try to at least think about what is happening
today.
Change is in the air, I feel it.
It's exhausting, but let's go back.
It's too hot out here."

"No, Marianna, look!
The sunset is turning red.
What's going on?"

The sky is solid red with baby cardinals.
The solid sky is moving, like birds glued together, turning and
twisting as one.
The sky is bending.
Una tormenta—the storm of discovery is on the way!
Birdies spark the roar and crash of thought.

Marianna and Joe under the pitch of the live sky find their way
back to the cabin.
Quiet and sober, they slide into bed.
Sex has no allure.
This will be their virgin night for shared dreaming.

Los pajaritos shower bravery on Joe and Marianna.
If birdies have flown their nests, if cardinals have become
murmurations of baby birds, if ZundelState quashes lovers of Art,
lovers of History.
If, if.
If, if.

Tonight's the night.
The air is perfect.
Humidity, perfect.
A big, beautiful, blank slate, big enough for two.

Junkyards?
Brain-O-Mats?
Agoras?
It's all noise.
Who cares.
Nighty night.

*

Abruptly, Joe and Marianna wake up.
They can barely grasp the night.
They open the cabin door and walk outside.
They wander around on the flat black landscape, wordless.
The earth is like a page.

A while later, Joe wanders back inside.
Everything there is ancient—every object, every single thing.
He takes out a bowl, pulls out a paper bag of flour, some baking
soda, salt, butter and milk, and begins to mix biscuit batter.

Marianna walks in the door, looks at Joe.
They mumble something to each other about food.
She takes newly hatched powder blue eggs from the cooler.
Lots of butter.
A grapefruit.

They remain silent.
Time barely moves.
In unison, they put together breakfast.

Marianna sets the wooden table.
Two chairs.
Two blue cloth napkins.
Ancient cutlery—forks, knives, spoons.

Joe and Marianna sit down to a meal from centuries past.
The nothingest thing turns out to be everything.
They are overwhelmed by sweetness.

The morning after their first duodream, Joe and Marianna
laze around for hours, aimless, like after a long night of rough sex.
They glance out the window but barely notice the scene.
Their duo-dream binds them closer.
It is almost too much.

By mid-afternoon, they begin to chat a little.
After a while, they mention the dream.

It was a grocery store.
Together in a "car," they drove to get there.
It was foggy and dark.
It was so beautiful.
It was a parking lot.
Spotlights lit up the airborne moisture.
Lots of other cars parked.
Low-lit and wet.
Such beauty made them breathless.
As they neared the supermarket door,
they felt fear of the Agora.

Inside now and flummoxed, they pushed a wire basket on wheels
as they walked up and down the aisles.
Sometimes Joe pushed it, sometimes Marianna.

Aisles of food in plastic.
Mozzarella covered in plastic.
Grapes in plastic bags.
Cashews in plastic.
Because Plastic Prohibitions had been in place for centuries,
seeing plastic terrifies them.

Finally they calm down.
"Do we need cornmeal?"
"Milk. We're almost out of milk."
As they consider items for purchase, torrential closeness rains on
them.

Back out in the glowing, moist parking lot, they feel glued
together.
Intimacy.

They awake.
It's the next morning.

*

As dreams were about to completely disappear off our planet,
there was a time when the line between dream and reality blurred.
As if a cloud of mist descended down onto cities, villages, and
valleys.
Was this a last gasp of humanness sprinkled on the earth by god
knows what?

5/ Pavel

&&&
Kern

A new person is standing there in the cabin with Joe and
Marianna.
Is he real?
Is he a figment of their minds?
A daydream?
There he stands, planted before them.
He stands for something.

Ah!
Is he the wise one from times gone by?
The Shaman bird.
Birdie.
FeatherMan.
A new person in their midst.
Pavel.

It is time for breakfast.
Joe pulls up a third chair.
They each consume a small bag of Fritos.
Then the three of them sit down to breakfast.

*

Pavel loved museums—he'd walk through them slowly, focusing,
taking in each historical item.
The era he lived in—centuries before Joe and Marianna—still
allowed the study of history, but only within the context and
confines of museums.

He particularly liked to visit a museum when he was on the verge
of flipping time up and down.
It helped to calm his fervent mind.
His favorite was the renowned Frito Pie Museum.

Now he is looking at the exhibits of the rise and decline of Frito
Pie and the central place it had in ancient culture.

Schools that served Frito Pie for lunch are listed.
Fragments of ancient lunch menus are on display: *pork roast, fish
shapes, Frito pie, corn pups, hot dogs, white rice, ham sand, egg sand,
grilled cheese sand, p.b. chews, sloppy joes, yellow cake.*
One room has cylindrical boxes that held salt: Diamond Crystal,
Kosher, and Morton.
When it rains, it pours, a sign says.
For years, scholars argued about what that meant.
Just reading the lunch menus helped his jelly-like legs turn strong
and solid.

Scholars believed that Frito Pie originated in a small
neighborhood called Texas where chili was one of the only foods
grown.
In one gallery, there's a diorama of a 7-Eleven shop with a
microwave cooker and a Mister Coffee machine and a rack with
replicas of different-sized bags of Fritos.
A worm-eaten text was discovered, and is temporarily on exhibit,
that refers to how a telephone repairman once walked into a
7-Eleven, bought a bag of Fritos and a can of chili, "microwaved
the chili, paid his tab, walked outside, slit the bag with a
pocketknife, poured chili over the Fritos, and ate his meal while
contemplating the traffic."
This is thought to be the origin of Frito Pie.
Taking all this in relaxes Pavel.

He leaves the museum and walks outside into the landscape.
A pond in the foreground, hills and castle behind.
A white bird stands in the water, watches Pavel.
Now is the time.
Pavel sucks in his breath.
He flips centuries backwards.
There he is, on a slow summertime morning in Greenport,
the Long Island, moseying to the hardware store with Albert Einstein.
"No!" he thinks, "I will go forward."
Time is one thing, past and future boomerang.
He flips time centuries forward.

When Pavel knocks at the cabin door, Marianna opens it.
"Who are you?" she says.
Now he finds himself eating biscuits and bacon with Marianna
and Joe.

The three of them finish breakfast and walk outside together.
Hills are covered in a profuse wildflower bloom.
Purple lupine.
Orange poppies.
A large lake.
Men rowing a green-shingled boat in and out of the tree branches.
Is that a man in the shadows?
He is holding up a huge tree by its trunk.
He is stronger than the world.
It's Mister Time.
He is moving towards the tree rowers.
The sky has turned a deep purple black.
The hills have turned white.
Joe, Marianna, and Pavel find themselves transfixed by a red
cardinal sky.

The couple feels threatened.
"Birds," Pavel says to them.
"Birds," replies Joe.
Pavel feels altogether iffy.
Marianna says "A bird," altogether confused.

*

It is 3090.
And so Pavel reappeared on this very earth, as he had been when
he ran through the woods over five hundred years ago.
Now, though, no forests.

Time's domains had merged into one.
Whatever was, still is.
Whatever will be, will return.

He has made the couple's acquaintance.

Pavel begins to tell them how in his time hundreds of years earlier,
dreaming had nearly died out.
The brain section that produced dreaming was nearly extinct, as
were toes and appendixes.

Because it seemed that the voice box was beginning to vanish,
some experts predicted that people were soon going to give up on
uttered speech.
Pavel described the quiet world that people thought was coming.

The world quiet.
No more tongues.
No eating.
No chewing.
No voice box.
No talking.

168

Singing?

No.

To think that something was once called the Talking Cure.

Both Joe and Marianna are transfixed by Pavel's vast knowledge.

Pavel told Marianna and Joe how he thought people would look
back on the era of uttered speech.

Each person had a voice box.

People sang songs, people yelled and cried—they whooped for
happiness!—people mumbled, stuttered, enunciated, they talked.
People talked all the time and it was a sound common to hear.
Sometimes it was a good sound, a steady hum of people going
back and forth with their minds, other times it was a bad sound—
chatter chatter chatter—busy, unpleasant, meaningless.
Mostly, it was in between.

People would say things to each other like:

How are you?
I am fine and you?

or longer

Nice day, huh?
Yeah, finally, after all that rain.
What a relief!

or even longer

What's for dinner?
What do you want?
I don't know.
What about meatloaf?
Might be good.

169

With mashed potatoes?
Yeah. Let's have that.
Yum.

*

As Marianna and Joe listen to Pavel lecture on what might have happened but didn't, silence overcomes them both.
Their threads of intimacy are wearing thin.

And as Marianna and Pavel meet on the threshold of time, they both sense their familial connection—each with their piercing, darting blue eyes.
"Oh you," she says to Pavel as Chopin's melancholy nocturnes soar in her head.
Pavel gazes into Marianna's eyes.
Is the magnetism love or family?
She carries the same Einstein dream genes, the two are bound.
Bound by blood and bound by purpose.

&&&
Marianna

I love Joe, you know that.
I am drawn to his opposition to ZundelState, his search for the secret.
I admire him so much.
He is so dashing.
He will do absolutely anything to uncover truths about ZundelState.
This is more than I can comprehend sometimes.

When I first met Pavel, I was blown away.
His lightness, his airiness.
In his presence, I heard the chirping of songbirds.
As if he was airborne.
He was made of matter so dreamy, so free, he could fly.
Joe was the ground in all its fertile, wide-ranging glory.
Pavel was the sky.

*

I understand that dreams still have a chance to make a comeback, to survive.
I understand I have a role in this.
It's my Einsteinian heritage, the long line of DNA I possess.
Humanness.
Pavel and I share a mission.

The technology that registers self-scales does not register dreams.
Don't ask me why.
The HistoryShit Division cannot track them.

It's pretty astounding.
What I mean is: dreams are feathery.
Vertraumt.
Dreams slip away like air.

Dreams are the escape.
Dreams are flight.
Dreams are los pajaritos abandoning the nests.
Dreams might save us all.
Will I follow Pavel into the sky?

&&&
Kern

Joe wanders away, scours the ground, rooted to the earth, to
history, to the past.
Is duo-dreaming on his mind?

Marianna and Pavel meander over to sit under a huge dark shade
tree.
She begins, she opens, she confides.
"One night, I think I was fourteen, it was summer—I was falling
into a deep sleep, I could hear a sound, a sound I had never heard
before.
Did I actually hear it?
Oh, it was my ukulele.
Someone strumming "Party Favor" on my uke.
Or was it somehow taking place in my brain?
When I fell into total sleep, feeling pictures moved through my
vision—hard to explain.
Pictures like clay, like longing, like butterflies, like flight.
When I woke up, nothing.
Irretrievable.
This haunted me for a few years.
How did those pictures get into my head?
But they too dissipated.
I was back to my numb self.

"I never told a soul.
A few years passed before it happened again.
Again, though, it was summer.
I can't talk about it."

Pavel touched her arm.
Pavel touched her hair.
He looked down at her face.
She looked up at his, unsure.
Like birds, like flight, like breath.
Nests.
It didn't take long for him to say "I have always been in love with you."

*

Meanwhile Joe, as he ambles off, fills with deep-ranging thoughts about the birdies.
Los pajaritos.
Like it's a physical attack—but why?—he has a sudden, intense desire to revisit the ArtFields.
The ArtFields will comfort him.
How daunting to travel such distance.
Now Joe Gulogulo, the wolverine, calls upon his highly developed animal-like traits.
Now, caribou-like, he sets out, a migrant.

In a fugue state, on and on he travels.
The travel seems endless—is it thousands of miles?—but his determination does not flag.
Eventually he sees the ArtFields up ahead.
His relief is boundless.
Finally, he reaches holy ground.

Upon entrance, he heads straight to Blue Poles.
Splatters everywhere!
Thank god.
On the trees, on the ground—dripping!
Red and yellow vines wrapping around them.

White birds perched on branches.
Chirping, twittering, singing.

The symphonic birdsong entices him in mysterious ways.
Such complex music!
Such life!
He is overcome by a wish to live here.
To splatter paint around.
To become a permanent element of the ArtFields.
He keeps looking up at the birds.

He begins to sing a low, slow song, "Swing low, sweet chariot, coming for to carry me home, swing low, sweet chariot, coming for to carry me home."

He starts to rip bird shapes out of heavy white paper.
He affixes one to a blue pole, now another.
Now another.
"This is the life," he mumbles to the birds.
Their singing intensifies.
He affixes a bigger one to another pole.
He can't stop.
He will change the blue pole forest to a Birdland.
Nothing will get in his way.

Is Marianna on his mind?
Is the intensity of their duodream fueling him?
One can't tell.
Twittering songbirds sing to the paper birds.

*

Marianna can't fathom where Joe has gone, but she has been overtaken by Pavel, their common mission.

She is sad and she is full.
Pavel looks at Marianna's quizzical face, a fleshy coral.
Careless love.
I ran all night long craving you.

Cows moo on the hill.
A line of robed men hold offerings.
Anything to free this constriction of the human heart.

Weather changes.
Piles of rubble, piles of grit blow in the wind.
Only Marianna and Pavel.
A bird alights on an elephant.
Now one alights on a camel.

He says to her, "You hold one end of the prayer flag and I'll hold
the other. Don't let go. Let the air breathe through. Then we will
repair to bed."

Something is stopping him.
She's transfixed.
She touches his thigh, everything burns inside.
Past and future mix.
They have to have sex.

He unbuttons his shirt, disrobes.
She wraps herself in a soft coral shawl.
He has given up on clothes, while she requires a covering.

The two walk down the hill, sit beside the pond.
They look to be very far away.
They look to be discussing something important.
It is impossible to hear what they are saying.
Are they talking about Joe?

Now Pavel looks to be flummoxed, looks back and forth, up
and down, as if he is awaiting someone or something that is not
arriving.
Marianna starts to weep.

This is disconcerting.
Marianna is afraid to touch Pavel.
He is like live electricity.
His eyes are so blue.
Crows are cawing as if on a mission.

As the narrator of this story, I am wondering what that mission is.
As the reader of this story, perhaps you know or wonder too.
If only you knew and there was a way you could tell me, I'd give
anything.

*

Oh!
A bird on the ceiling in the palace bedroom!
Marianna and Pavel in a canopy bed beneath the singing bluebird.
Time is truly nothing.
Chirping bluebirds are flitting across the red ceiling.

An elephant in the sky with many trunks.
A bird on the ground.

Suddenly all is three-dimensional.

&&&
Marianna

"Pavel, last week a weird thing happened when I was at work,
sitting at my desk, going over the self-scales.
A tiny, furry mouse appeared on the floor.
It was so small, maybe it had just been born.
It was larger than a golf ball and smaller than a tennis ball.
I watched it explore the room.
It was so cute!
It was curious and new.
It took my attention away from work."

"Why is this weird?" asked Pavel.

"A mouse?
At work?

"I started to think of how to get rid of the live little creature.
Poison it?
Kill it in a mousetrap?
Put it in the icy outside where it would slowly suffer and die?
Killing it seemed so sad.

"I was torn.
Killing seemed sad.
At that moment, my machine crashed.
This has never happened.
I do understand how crucial dissolve-to-kill is for ZundelState to
flourish the way it does.

"Just then my boss swept in and offered me a cider doughnut.
We chatted, we chewed.
Then she asked me to leave work.
She suggested I take a few days off.
She could not have been nicer.

"Pavel, why are you looking at me like that?"

"You are in danger, Marianna!
The birdies have flown the nest.
We must take to the sky."

&&&

Kern

The two are flying over hills as if they are winged.
One leads, then the other.
Now they are looking down at the Junkyards from a great height.
Now they are passing over the ArtFields.
A crowd of cardinals fly on either side of them, shielding them,
making a holy space.
The birds appear purposeful.
They fly over an assembly of men robed in garments of carmine,
crimson, maroon.

Blue sky punctuated by red birds, red-robed men, green hills.
The men look up at the bold sight of the two airborne creatures.
With long-fingered hands outstretched, the men appear to be
making an offering.
Some of them hold books.

Is this real or a dream?
The line between is fine.
It is neither real nor dream, it's in between.

The robed men disrobe.
Standing naked, arms still outstretched.
Some walk away.
Beneath a great, leafy tree, they find shade.

They are passing around a pipe.
As Pavel glides lower, the smoke attracts him.
Marianna follows until they both reach the ground.
Into the distance, the birds fly on.

*

A minuet.

Pavel is dragging his feet.
Ah! Now a harpsichord is resounding throughout the halls!
The notes come on fast, right on top of each other.
Pavel smiles a faint smile.
Time is playing tricks on the two of them.
Are they on the same plane?
Are they together or not?

Is five hundred years keeping them separated?
Too many notes all at once.

*

Marianna falls asleep, dreaming of horses crossing the flooding
lake.
There's an island with boulders and bare trees.
Eighteen white birds perch on the highest branches, looking back
at her.
Two fly off.
Gone.
A hunter with a long gun silently shoots tigers.
A mother bird observes.

It looks like a tableau—in the foreground, a caribou, the sky
layered lavender and blue.
Everything thuds to a standstill.
Hunters rest their spears, dismount their horses.
The birds settle down.
Time is flexing its slowness.

Prayer flags, strung from trees, rage and flap in the glacial wind.
Dark indigo clouds crowd the howling, drooping sky.
Everywhere, water is rising.
Trees look like lace.
Rivers have no banks at all.
Space abounds, expands.

*

Ka-roo. Ka-roo.
Witnesses.
History takers.

Pavel actually does have wings, maybe.
I don't know but maybe so.
I truly can't tell.
Under his thin shirt are feathers.

A king on horseback, a falcon perched on his hand.
The sky, blue—the earth, mustard-colored.

Now Marianna and Pavel, lying in bed after fragile, turbulent
love-making—there, the two of them, wordless.
Staring at the painted ceiling of paralyzed birds on the wing.

They rest.
They have had their separate dreams.
They will arise and sit outside in the thin blue air, its warmth, and
each, separately, dwell within their separate dreams.

Marianna knows what it is like to duodream.
This is not that.
It is painful for her to picture Joe settling in to a life in the
ArtFields.
The lake has many ducks swimming.

The dreamworld has taken Marianna and Pavel in,
for better or worse.
The sky turns to a paisley pattern.
Marianna is in disarray.

There is too much writing in the sky to behold.
Birds fly through the letters.
There are clouds of pages.
Horses clop by, riderless.
It's incomprehensible.
Into the air, she waves a white handkerchief.

Acknowledgements

Jamali-Kamali: A Tale of Passion in Mughal India, Mapin Publishing, Ahmedabad, India, 2011.

Thanks to Igor Greenwald for the use of his photo on Page 101.

Heartfelt thanks to the following people who contributed to this volume in crucial ways:

O.P. Jain—founder of Sanskriti Pratishan, supporter of the restoration of the Jamali-Kamali Mosque and Tomb

Jaya Sanskrityayana Parhawk—resident manager at Sanskriti, answered my constant questions

Bruce Wannell—Mughal scholar, generous source of research

Didi Goldenhar and Jeffrey Harrison—fellow poets, invaluable critics

Milo Beach, Rennie McQuillkin and Bipin Shah—instrumental in the Indian publication of *Jamali-Kamali*

Joy Johannessen—editor extraordinaire (*ZundelState*)

Todd Portnowitz—champion adviser

Paul Graubard—my husband and first reader, always

To the memory of Jonathan Matson, my literary agent, who stood by me to follow art's circuitous route, no matter where it led.

About the Author

KAREN CHASE is the author of two collections of poems, *Kazimierz Square* and *BEAR*, as well as *Jamali-Kamali: A Tale of Passion in Mughal India*, a book-length homoerotic poem, published in India in 2011. Her award-winning book, *Land of Stone*, tells the story of her work with a silent young man in a psychiatric hospital where she was the hospital poet.

In her memoir *Polio Boulevard*, Chase brings the reader back to the polio outbreak of the 1950s that crippled our country. In her lively sickbed she experiences puppy love, applies to the Barbizon School of Modeling, and dreams of Franklin Delano Roosevelt. *The Larooco Log: FDR on the Houseboat*, a project that grew directly out of her memoir, follows Franklin Delano Roosevelt during a Florida winter when he lived on a houseboat, attempting to regain use of his paralyzed legs. *History Is Embarrassing*, her collection of essays, came out in 2024.

Karen Chase's poems, stories and essays have appeared in *The New Yorker*, *The New Republic*, *The Gettysburg Review* and *Southwest Review*, among others. Her poems have been anthologized in *The Norton Introduction To Poetry*, Andrei Codrescu's *An Exquisite Corpse Reader*, and Billy Collins' *Poetry 180*. Chase and her husband, the painter Paul Graubard, live in Western Massachusetts.

Also by Karen Chase

Kazimierz Square
(poetry)

Land of Stone
Breaking Silence Through Poetry

BEAR
(poetry)

Jamali Kamali
A Tale of Passion in Mughal India
(poetry)

Polio Boulevard
(memoir)

FDR on His Houseboat
The Larooco Log, 1924–1926

History Is Embarrassing
(essays)

Printed by Imprimerie Gauvin
Gatineau, Québec